Winter Wonderland 2023

Bindweed Anthology

Heavenly Flower Publishing

Winter Wonderland 2023: Bindweed Anthology

First published as a collection December 2023

Content copyright © 2023 Heavenly Flower Publishing authors
Edited by Leilanie Stewart

ISBN: 9798870785622

Bindweed Magazine: https://bindweedmagazine.com
Heavenly Flower Publishing: heavenlyflowerpublishing@gmail.com
Find us on Facebook: https://fb.me/BindweedMagazine

Cover design by Leilanie Stewart

BINDWEED ANTHOLOGY

WINTER WONDERLAND
2023

HEAVENLY FLOWER PUBLISHING
AUTHORS

CONTENTS

EDITOR'S NOTE

As this is an anthology, there may be some content that is troubling for some readers. Content disclaimer for reader discretion: adult themes.

Bindweed proudly features writers from all over the English-speaking world., therefore there may be differences in spelling and punctuation, and even in meaning.

POETRY

Martin Christmas

Abandoned Glove

One.
One handed poker.
One upmanship.
One for the road.
One too many drinks.
One and only.
One way.
One life.

As Dylan
(not Thomas)
put it,

'One too many mornings
and a thousand
miles
behind.'

The sound of one glove clapping
and somewhere . . .
you.

Moth

Small insignificant moth
resting on a leaf
while this giant being
lords over it with his
camera.

In reality, moth, you are
the god who descended from above
to show the other being
that it is earthbound
while you have the gift of
flight.

Ed Ahern

Stadium Cheer

Waiting in line is the insult
that introduces me to the injury
of compression into a stadium crowd.
Forced to watch a jumbotron
because players are too far below
to discern nuance of movement.
Inflicted with a cold hot dog
that smells of unknown mammal.
Abusive ambient noise forcing me
to scream into a conversation.
And when released from confinement
degenerating into bellicosity
as a parking lot road warrior.

Visitations

My son arrived just now, his son in tow.
Our meetings are too few to keep abreast
of how our lives have shifted tone and flow
and how we had to change as we were stressed.

The love still shared was born with traits now faux
yet it abides in changeling sympathy.
Our differences are gulches set below
the bridging skeins of trust and empathy.

For there's no judgement shown by we who know
we cannot let the facts malform the true,
its basking warmth enabling us to glow
in spite of lives that wandered off askew.

Erin Jamieson

Thaw

it's warmer today
buttery sun stretching
like a sleepy cat

but this light is
more than we expected
and after months of snow
we find it unbearable

to see stains on our walls,
fingerprint smudges on our windows
our faded engagement photos

it will be better when it's warm
we said
we won't feel the need
to destroy one another

but now the snow is melting
and we understand how alone
we really are

how barren our yard is
stripped trees, our failed garden
there's nothing left to hide
our failures, no bitter cold
to numb our senses.

If Only

I capture thunder
in a mason jars
under dusky stars
fingers blistering
from absence of

sun- I only come out
at night now, only
under storm clouds
where you are inside
somewhere, holding her
and telling her stories
of how the fireflies looked
as you danced in muddy
grounds- our stories,
regurgitated, reinvented
to become magical to
eclipse this moment.

Erin Jamieson

C.L. Liedekev

A Season Behind

My lover was born
with chronic velvet eyes.

She danced hind-up into a Virginia
folk concert, dragging her naked skin
past Wolf Trap Road, past me
then through me,

making my vision dip yellow to blue,
blinking away a sunset
as the brown of her form
left me a season behind

as a walking stick under new snow

In morning,
she pulled on her shirt
in an act she called her field dressing.
I could smell the echo
                of her tobacco fingers
sweet at buttonbush
like piles of Jersey hay.

They buttoned my jeans last,
fingers nimble,
feet still covered deep
in reddish mud.

Now way I knew the cells were already growing inside her.

On the ride home,
car smell and joy,
my grandmother's issues returned
as broken teeth,
as the river's end of a mouth,
a collarbone snapped like antlers.

I bolted to her, heavy,   sure-foot over
the Tacony–Palmyra,

but Penn Med,
where she lay in the status of a reality,

the same reality that the Penn Med steps
met for me,
ignoring the elevator, the concrete
not informing my forehead, my knee,
foot gone backward
in a desperate rush.

I lay in the stairwell,
next to the foot-worn edge,
the pain pulling through me,
chanting, crying,
in the same voice as my grandmother,

and a voice I would never know.

The Crockpot Broke on The Kitchen Floor

The nightmare: black hulk of ceramic smashed
like the snap of our backyard oak in Hurricane Gloria.
The explosion pushed back my wooden chair,
its lilac cover sliding under my desperate body.
My mother walked out the screen door.

My father walked back into the kitchen
I imagined him dead, slicked in brown gravy.
Greasy, his throat open pink, a cut of meat,
he is singing. Voice garbled as mushy potato
after potato is pushed through the wound,
a sliding avalanche, showing me
that every escape comes
with a price.

The smell of onions, brown and Irish-boiled stains
streaked blue cabinets. I remembered
tendrils on the wedge of wood
across the table, moving at me, steam rising
from oily water's skin.

The spear of carrot, the snapped pot edge
like broken stones of a temple.
The sacrifice long since dried and invisible.

In this picture

there can be only one mother.
One that handles fire.
One that has arms formed into braces.
Holds the walls, keeps the Family Stone
playing in the living room.

In the days of the Jersey breaking,
the street outside our house would
fill with kids and hockey nets.
The screams a dull seance as she dances.

The windows open, screens ripped down
like blinking eyes.
The curbs begin to hum to the front steps,
to a man who drove all night to get home.

The sound of the truck door closing.
Engine shuts off. Keys fall into jeans pocket.
Boots on cement and sliding outcomes -
One that's done all the things you set out to do.

Casserole becomes a choir,
the drum of soft hands on ceramic,
rhythm and feet slide past an opening door.
It has been three weeks, everything smells

like the summer, like arrival,
like nothing ever happened,
like when I drop my hockey stick
all her wounds will close smooth
and this night is not a final stand.

Sister of Splinters

The tunnel that
was my sister's sobriety collapsed,
bone hands pulled her inside,
buried her in the warped
floorboards of my grandmother's
house. At night she
pulled splinters from the wood
and decorated her tongue
in the Irish words for lies.

The moon smashed across
the siding like an errant
boyfriend's ring. The silver
stain of reflection trickled
into the window, drained
through the rug, down into
the pyre's cherry heart.
The myth that pain gets
you higher is passed around
the room.

As the thump and growl
melted into day, my sister
reformed at the kitchen table.
Her head rolled off bullshit
into guillotine form. As if
the sky was not redder,
the walls wetter, food made
in bowls uneaten, lips
peeled in long ropes
along the inescapable
well of her mouth.

The Girl in the Maytag Box

She was a woman
born of big words, of mixed birth,
a wives' tale her mother spoke
in hushed clenched teeth, her daddy
a trowel in the dirt, all steel, and stab.
She loved him that way, broken and warn
like the Street Road blacktop after a storm,
petrichor mixing with the death throw
of worms. Freedom is built on his
exterminator grind. Made whole
in the sun by her mother's dyed hair.

When she was five, she curled up
in the empty washer box, its brown
walls leveled with the names of bird gods,
of green mountains where every
edge is snapped into divots.
of a moon that held her close, yellow,
shine and armor. She dreamt
of knowing the key to every word,
their outlines a penumbra, their spaces
windows to new flowers beyond
the daises that mom picked off the road.

Each time she wakes, phosphenes
and lightning, falling glass, and fear
along the edge of her eyes. The dark
of the box holds more minotaurs
than ministers, has the grave walls,
the sky missing all its stars, eaten,
fallen, fingered clean. She crawls
to find the same night, the same day,
a carpet's touch as safe as any love.

The sound

is in my chest,
down to my spare
tire, fat hair burial
of fear, bit nails
and Cocoa Pebbles.
Vine seed shifts
up through my chest,
up coffee burnt
esophagus, off
the weight of drunken
noodles, fat rock
in my throat. The
toad face of misery
unclenching.

Unclenching
the misery of toad face,
throat fat as a rock,
noodle off, a drunk noodle,
coffee burnt chest,
esophagus
of vine seeds,
shit of pebbles,
nails bit down to the burial,
fat with fear,
chest flat as a spare tire,
the sound is in me.

C.L. Liedekev

James Croal Jackson

Forest Song

Hide these holes from death's dentists.
Suburban wealth I heard is best eaten
slowly. We can be the beasts we were
warned against. My mouth and ear
are hollow. Follow endless footsteps
into forgettable forests. For this I sing
a song I hope you won't remember.

Summer Sputter

I like the way you hug you squeeze me
like an almost-empty ketchup bottle to
wring the last sputter of my worth. We
spent one laborious summer in the sun,
almost burnt in cigarettes. You walked
your boss's dog and your boss walked
you on trails we walked by the river.
Walked us. Communion with
the trees, canopy shade, we looked to
the river, in those moments endless.

The Sword of Light

This fixture you forgot
on your back patio.

You say you are confused—
how did that turn on? It has

been months since I last visited.
I say *the light is a metaphor*

for our friendship. Big plants
sit in chairs in your brown-fenced

garden. Don't know how close
to be anymore. Never get too close.

A tomato vine peeks from a planter
above you. Gardening's a hobby,

inching toward the *thirty* you fear.
An August birthday during the lost

summer and you toss a squeaky
blue ball in my general direction,

more wildly as the night goes on,
and Lola retrieves it every time.

You say she slept upstairs with
you for the first time. We joke

she didn't fall immediately, that you
had to tell her to turn the television

off, stamp her cigarette out. With our masks,
I only see your eyes smile. I hope you notice

mine. It is dark, as it has been for months,
and we try to stay illuminated, despite

these killer particles suspended
somewhere in the talk between us.

Framework

So, you caught
me dozing.
Our bed a compass
without direction.

We buy a home
we say will wrench
us from the dredges
we have been stuck

in, the blue head-
lights pointing up,
forever, the language
of our love.

Gold Hole

mosquito in the wind I itch my heavy
soil in the little dynamite world I in-
habit the ghost of some nonsense
brioche a thunderclap stumbling
down the wedding aisle in front
of family some worlds you never
lie about but break you must
pinch the nerve that binds you
and open the gold hole to the
masses that want to help let them.

You Ask What Home Means to Me

Home is a location. Not a house.
Because I live in a home to be near

my people. When I leave, my people
follow me to the next. Because home

is people, not place, though often
I want to live in a home hidden

by trees, where branch shadows
won't follow into where I live.

James Croal Jackson

Ben Macnair

Expectations

He was drunk,
the first time they met,
high on life,
intoxicated with expectation.
She thought he was a charmless bore,
she made no secret of her exasperation,
sitting with her friends,
a quiet night out, spoilt.
Sipping cheap red wine,
and talking about her day,
and her Friend's lives,
and how Sarah's Dad was killed,
a year ago tonight,
by a 19-year-old,
high on life
intoxicated with his new life,
celebrating freedom with his friends.
That late-night call,
a pool of blood,
and a lifetime of regret,
because he was drunk.

Meanwhile, the door slams, the container is sealed
and accountability begins.

My date says my face is pretty
but the pretty you find may hide an evil mind
even if you live on my blameless boulevard
with a sufficient number of barbershops.

I hear you now reside where irrigation has begun
and new farm methods introduced.

I know your existence is challenging
and may be risky and dangerous—
all processes secret.
Act accordingly.

I savor the fantasy of you being safe
and drinking a martini beside me
because martinis made you happy.

Rest assured, I won't let a garnish pervert
drop a piece of bacon or maraschino cherry in mine.

Words to the wise

Dear Pedro the Helpful Burro:

The September issue of *Boy's Life* was the best ever.
Nowhere have I been told so awesomely
why I have problems with jerky boys, creepy girls and dumb adults
(and I didn't have to look up as many words this time
to guess what you are trying to say).

That being so: Much was missing from your list of things to do,
like what a boy should look for and what we should believe is true.
For example, when you make fake faces and put on too much make up,
you hide your inner beauty -- if you have any.
How the lifesaver must quickly reverse position
to make sure his legs are well forward over his chest.

Maybe you should include my extremely important information
in the Hobby Hows or Think and Grin of your next issue.
I'd use the $5 suggestion pay to buy an ant house.
I'm really glad you finally pointed out what I know is so:
A lot of people are like Rupert the Invincible
and a lot of people are like Webelos Woody.
And that's the most deadly threat to the world today.

Another word to the wise, Pedro: Dental hygiene is important,
or so they preach to me over and over again.
So don't let too many carrots stay stuck in your teeth.

Your friend for today and forever,
The future St. Francis de Sales, bearer of 89 merit badges.

Paul Brucker

Christine Emmert

Ice

I froze
a long time ago
after sunny insults of youth.
Feel my smoothness
and my rigidity
under your thawed kisses.

Lynn White

The Spirit of Christmas to Come

The ghost slid down the rabbit hole
on a dark wintery night.
He expected to arrive in Wonderland
if such a place exists
and he believed it did,
just as he believed in ghosts and Santa Claus.
There was a full glass on a table.
He looked for a label saying: "Drink Me".
But there was no label. So he drank it anyway.
It left a nice warm feeling inside him,
"spirit for the spirit", he laughed aloud.
There was a plate of pastries.
He looked for a label saying: "Eat Me",
but there was no label. So he ate them anyway,
He lay back contentedly
then smiled somewhat sheepishly
at the old man dressed in red carrying a large sack
who was looking none too pleased at the scene.
"Well", said the ghost,
"Anyone can mistake a chimney for a rabbit hole."

Joseph Farley

Risks to the Traveler

I try to watch the road when I drive,
But it keeps moving,
Trying to get out of the way
Of cars
Racing
In haphazard motion.

If asphalt and concrete
Gets so perturbed,
Why shouldn't
The pilot and passengers
Seek to get
Off the highway?

Give me an old train
From the forties or fifties,
Coal smoke, diesel,
Or wound with a spring,

So we can all relax
As we get to
Where we are going.

We can all still
Bounce and cry
And scream together
If it goes off the track.

Broken Bed

The bed is broken.
It sags to one side.
Springs stick up
Through the mattress
And tear at
Sleeping skin.

Why do I lay in it?
Why not throw it
Out in the trash,
Acquire a new one
That's more comfortable
And supportive
Of my spine?

It is not a question
Of money.
I am sure I could find
A bargain somewhere.

What is it
About this bed
That makes me
Keep it?

Is it an addiction
To suffering?
Or is it just
Laziness?

Or is it something
Different altogether,
A question of memories
Known now only
To me
And an old mattress,
Bedspring and frame?

I wonder while I lay here
Bleeding again,
With so many old moments
Of pleasure and pain
Mingling
With just the pain that is left.

Discernment

Tell me the truth,
Or tell me a lie.

How would I know
The difference?

Trust is a fault
We all share,

But it's too hard
To doubt

Everything
\All the time.

It would put us
On edge,

Make us fearful
Of every interaction.

Let's just say
You're the victor
On this occasion.

On another
I may prevail.

It is better to ignore
The small cuts,
The small losses,

Than wind up
With no one

Around when
You need them.

Even the devil
Can throw you a bone,

Even an angel
Can stomp on your head.

That Certain Something

The only one I understood
Sat in the back of the class
Half asleep or half awake.

She clearly heard more
Than the professor's lecture
And the lame reports
From other students.

We never talked.
That might have ruined it,
Made perceptions
Turn out to be
The illusions
They usually are.

I saw her in that class
And one other,
No more after that.

She had that certain something.
It might have been contagious,

Or again, simply nothing,
A trick of hope
And belief.

I wonder what
ever happened to her?

Not really.
I didn't even care
Enough

To ask her
Her name.

All The Missiles And Melting Ice

All the missiles and melting ice
Won't prevent the sun from rising
Over a world with or without
Cities built by ant-like men.

Parched by fire, nuclear or carbon based,
The Earth will continue.
Life will go on, existing in some form
Whether or not we are here
To witness it.

Take my hand and I'll take yours.
We will share this last dance,
With or without music.
What we have now is what we have.
When we are gone, so we are gone.

Let's not trouble ourselves
About ghosts or spirits,
Where we will be or won't be.
We smiled for a while,
Laughed and loved.

We do not need to see the credits.
Walk out of the theater
Or turn off the set.

Everything fades. So what?
Remember you can't fade
Unless you were light to begin with.

Joseph Farley

L. Sydney Abel

Hush

There's diamonds in her eyes. A kiss upon her lips. A finger upon her mouth, saying hush now don't you speak.

If I was a brook I'd stay, but I'm a sea with the sun upon me. I'm not what you think. I'm not a truthful boy. I'm a cheating species, dying on a different shore.
I can be a lying Billy, or him which Fate's hand purposely hid. I'm forever a page torn. I'm a satirical moon. I'm sunlight on cold water, showing scars unseen.

You Government

In the 50s and 60s *You* took children from mothers, putting suffering on those you called whores.
Now between mother and child are doors—some to remain forever closed.

You officious prats meddled with people's lives, wielding law-making knives.
Some for the better, some for the worse. Those suffered arrangements endure.
You broke the hearts of the pure. Many a passenger on a train, some get off, some remain.

Speaking figuratively: Those grown-up kids should take those meddlesome prats and hang them with bureaucratic chain. Watch them swing for each and every mistake, never to be made again and when dead drop them in the deepest lake.

What's the point in payback? The damage is done. Apologise You Government for your mistakes, for all those mothers and children's sakes.

Time of life has imposing trickery—*You* Government.
No more fakery—*You* Government.
Show the mystery—*You* Government.
Open the history—*You* Government…

Jim Conwell

Old

The old were the ones who told the stories and were consulted when a particular kind of wisdom was needed but now we're sick of their endless bloody ramblings. They used to do essential tasks that could be done sitting down. They're still sitting on their arse and we're spending vast sums of money to keep them there. If only they would fade out quickly and quietly.

Only, I am old.
But I'm certainly not finished here.
It's bad enough that life's an impossible task but then to also be told at some arbitrary moment *Okay, time's up*.

You might think *Well, what the **fuck** was that all for!*

Adjustments

I do know some normal people – well-defended neurotics. Not that I mean to be derogatory, it's a useful adaptation. Well-defended neurotics get on pretty well. As if the world was made for them.

What some unfortunate people cobble together though
is only thin and frightening.
Others have extravagant success but in specialised areas.

Take Hitler, for example, sick enough to be spectacularly successful in a certain sphere; the one that provoked and fed a collective madness. Like it or not, he was a master of that.

The pathologies we are capable of can be quiet and unassuming and they can be spectacular. Mine is the quiet and unassuming type. But that's from the outside. Don't come in here because, in here, it's a lot weirder than that.

My Father is Dead

I know
that all the things I understand
about me and my father
are not true.

When my truths
met the truths of others,
we would have to see,
painful as it is,
that it's all lies.

Only life is the truth. Only that.

My father is dead and
available now for anybody's use.

Chugging

I know this is not light stuff. I know that.
And it goes on and on and on. I know that.
And that's not what people like. I know that, too.
I'm not saying I know it all. I'm just saying.

I don't know shit, that's what my Dad believed.
Or I know a lot about the wrong things.
Things nobody who was right should know.
I didn't know what I needed to know.
That's what he thought.

I believe he was right.
Too much thinking, that's what did it.

I started thinking when I woke up in the morning
and only stopped when I went to bed. Nowadays,
even going to bed doesn't stop me thinking.
I just go on thinking using a different engine.
The day time one rests and the night one –
which runs on heavy diesel – takes over.

Chugging through all kinds of shit
till I wake up again and start back
with the unleaded-fuel one.

Out of Bounds

I remember sitting in there, though I can't imagine that anybody would have
brought something to sit on and it was always a damp place. It gave a secret view
of the comings and goings in a place even more forbidden to us. We had crossed
into a resistance unknown to the priests and masters whose authority was absolute
everywhere else. Perhaps too, we understood instinctively that they had shot
themselves in the foot with their arbitrary prohibitions. By forbidding us to be there,
they had ensured that it could only be secret. Once, we were nearly caught when a
prefect appeared at the edge of the copse. There was a moment of panic until we
realised he was too far away to be able to identify us. He shouted for us to stop
and he came running. All that propelled him though, was the affront that our
continued flight paid to his authority. What propelled us was knowledge of the
consequences of being caught there and so Hermes gave flight to *our* heels. I did
not know then, that Zeus' son was a god of transitions and boundaries, far less that
he is patron and protector of literature and poets. I only knew the glorious flight as
he lifted our feet and the gap between us and the prefect grew. There would come
a moment when we had to stop, straighten our ties and our hair and blend back in
with the other boys, hoping no one noticed our breathlessness until it could
subside. There was something else there too, in that leaf-mould place. A certain
stillness in the air. A kind of silent expectation. So that, filled with it, you would not
run when the prefect shouted but wait there on the spot for him to arrive and push
a knife into his soft stomach with one hand behind his head to prevent him from
drawing back, to lean him in towards the murder of this place, to leave him there
with the hilt sticking from his cooling body and to wash your hands in the sink and
go in to supper.

Disadvantaged

I can drink coffee because
I just make the order, it arrives
and some money disappears
from my bank account.

For the moment,
that need not worry me.
For many people that's not so.

We live alongside each other.

How is this possible? Historical precedent.
Anything seems normal if it's normal.
It's a survival mechanism.
It has seen us through slaughter, pestilence
and starvation.
We certainly would not
have arrived here without it.

But it does have disadvantages.

Right now I am lucky
to be on the right side of them.

Jim Conwell

Robert Estes

Empathy Pang

It was more curse
than privilege to witness
(accidentally to have caused)
my child's new understanding
that time when she was only five.

I took her
to Kubrick's *Barry Lyndon*
when it was new.
In a scene well into the film
the title character's pride and joy
his young son
lies terribly injured in bed,
asks his father
if he is going to die.
His father reassures him:
No, you're not going to die.

Suddenly the scene shifts
outdoors to a rumbling wagon
in a rustic funeral procession.
My little girl grabs my arm
and urgently asks
"What's happening?!"
Stunned a bit myself,
I tell her they're taking
the boy to his grave.

*"But his father told him
he wasn't going to die!"*

She'd been the *child*
—not the parent—in that scene!
I hadn't appreciated
the treasure of innocent trust
in parents' power and truth
she still conserved.
The guilt of revelation
grips my memory yet.

Robin Ouzman Hislop

Cell Was Here

CELL
was here

was

was

was

was

was
here here here CELL here here
here

was here was was was was

you are just a simulation
& i am 10 to the power bleep
a simulation more than you
let me cast you the pearls of fate
the entropy of entelechy
resource the body electric
engraved as epitaphs on the sacrificial altar's axe

fossilised hominoid chop chop suey
CELL was here CELL was here.

Mary Anne Abdo

A Bridge Over the East River

While few people remember my name.
History has recorded my contribution to this engineering marvel.
Being a woman in Victorian society.
Higher education was unacceptable.
A woman's place was behind her husband.
A twist of fate granted me the grace of a man's only world entrance.
Having to tend to my husband's decompression illness.
Finding my way through the curriculum of engineering.
Mastering this educational maze of steel and stone.
I, a woman assumed the task as chief engineer.
Enduring a decades worth of snide contractors.
Inspectors, politicians, reporters sneering in my face.
It was not until that last year my reputation garnered respect.
Did you know I was the first person to cross the Brooklyn Bridge?
In a carriage with my red rooster for good luck!
That feat gained attention to those far and wide.
That all my womanly efforts were so monumental.
I am, Emily Warren Roebling.
I am the woman who saved the Brooklyn Bridge.

The Defunding of Humanity
I can't
I just can't participate.
In a countdown of another human being's horrid demise.
Demise by the hands of five human beings sworn to "serve and protect."
I think of Rodney King in this moment, images still emblazoned in my mind.
A second before shutting off that dreadful noise box invention.
Shaking and shuttering again, over a snippet of another beating.
A once vital Tyre.
He is now reduced to a beyond battered human rubble.
No one is perfect; this world is not made for perfection.
Police work can be social work.
Ripping apart another's countenance is not a solution.

Solutions are made with clearer thoughts.
Finding ways to garner assistance.
Listening to the CBS Sunday morning program.
The commentator asking;
"Why?
For what?
Are we now back to our post-pandemic lull?
Why is congress slow to right the wrongs of society?
Are they maybe too busy to comprehend the magnitude of this division in our country?"
And yet, I am writing another prose of protest.
Protesting, that my poetry should not include cruelty!

Mary Anne Abdo

Christina Chin and Paul Callus

Spring Festival

spring festival
the stress of weight
on the scales
  the crumbling
  of resolutions

Hot chamomile

hot chamomile
in a bone china teapot
mistral wind whistles
  a vagrant panhandles
  outside the restaurant

Jane Rosenberg LaForge

Illustrated Rage

For one glorious week before
I turned 17, I rode around
town with a couple of boys,
one driving, the other slinging
an arm around my neck, shoulders,
or my waist, anywhere his skin might
make aberrant contact with my nerves
and sweat, inspire a real conflagration
in the back seat, or with his ex.
We were all at a party when she stole
my steady, setting off a chain reaction
that would engulf not only the couples
involved but also bystanders who spread
accounts of the damage as though it
was the equivalent of contraband, or
words scrawled on sacred tablets.
I'd known the boyfriend thief's
beaux since elementary school,
when I was cowardly and awkward,
and he was a few years older, beloved
for his artistic talents; his parents
were famous animators, creators
of a show I now watch with my daughter
because its themes and characters
are considered relatable even decades
afterward. It was never clear how the car
was obtained nor who owned it, because
the model had been ritually shamed in
the national media for its volatile design
and the manufacturer's refusal to remove
it from the market. Hundreds if not thousands
prowled and punctuated the city streets
as though this behavior was to be expected.
We cruised into parking lots, supermarket
and mall garages, loading zones or anywhere
we could feel the power of being seen,
counted, remembered for the risks we
took at the expense of our parents'
ambivalence. I would rue the day I lost
my reputation, my father conjectured,

but the truth was I wanted nothing more
than to be consumed in a car filled with
boys, my remains inextricable from theirs,
our final embrace so ruthlessly public.

Between Enthusiasms

When the world ends it will be beautiful;
I know because it was this, once earlier,
in the autumn I was between apartments
or was it boyfriends, or eruptions from
the volcano in the Philippines, or it had
to have been in Indonesia. The atmosphere
was seeded with primordial contents,
and that everything that had been beyond
the normally inaccessible was enhanced,
available at my doorstep. The blue hum
of embers on the verge of catching; rinds
of citrus as they curled inward and purpled
the surface and became impervious to judgment;
all the high and dissonant elements of chance,
spontaneous courage and studied cowardice;
what cannot be controlled but perhaps harnessed,
despite the best efforts of scientists and engineers
to tame them as if they were horses, peeling away
their wild veneer without damaging their nobility
and intelligence. In truth the air had been shaken
as much as the earth, and it could no longer conceal
its mechanics as I worked for my father, managing
the wholesale destruction of potential woodlands.
We celebrated the end of each workday with decadent
meals I knew would give me nightmares, consumed
so close to bedtime. But I was done with dreams;
with mopping up and public relations, and ready
to dive into any fire revealing its phases in a similar
dance of stains and vapors, so long as it started
before I could land on my next enthusiasm.

Time: Specific Standard

The past was supposed to be easier
to bear in Los Angeles, as it was abated
by other people's bliss, small victories
like our mother removing birds' nests
whole and without injury to the infrastructure
of stick and lint the birds appropriated
from the discontents of our washer/dryer
system. Just below the weeping bottlebrush
tree, the leavings of the laundry my mother
said had to be boiled for the sake of
hygiene and public decorum, mixed
with milkweed and nettles that my sister
and I tried to make perfume with. In the alley
between apartment buildings, in the unit
my mother purchased for my father to settle
the last remnants of their marriage,
I used to listen for crickets and mockingbirds,
until I had the windows replaced with
high tech materials to make the temperature
inside the place tolerable, and subsequently
locked out all the sounds of other species.
Nothing to keep my mind from racing to
some inviolable finish, and in my hometown
I felt unwanted as when my body began changing
in ways that refused categories of obvious
and average, and I had to explain not only
what I was, but what I could become in a
future everyone was afraid of.

Jane Rosenberg LaForge

Brian Daldorph

On the road

My daughter slammed the door in my face and now I'm driving home.
I'd driven all night to say sorry to her, to ask her
to forgive the sins of a father who tries to love her—
I'm just not very good at it.

Hours and hours on the highway and all I can think about is
how I should have done things better--
what does it mean, *to do things better?*

I'm sitting in a gas station café. Grits
and eggs--don't even know if I'm hungry. My gut hurts,
I've got a killer headache from all those
5-hour energy drinks to keep me driving all night.

I've got to work double shift when I get home—I need the money.
My car's got a death rattle, I owe rent—Larry won't give me another break.

Soon I'll be back on the road, the road to nowhere.
No one will care if I make it there or not.

The last time I saw my father

The last time I saw my father was in Grand Central Station. He was explaining to me how the trains worked. He'd studied it not because he needed to but out of his own interest. He was like that, my dad, loved finding out about things, especially wonderful mechanical things like trains—they were mechanical the last time I saw him.

He said it's a miracle of coordination that so many trains enter and leave Grand Central in the way they do, and he began explaining the complexities of scheduling: "And just think if there's an error, just think of the consequences of one small error."

He'd sketched out some diagrams and charts he was keen to show me and though I tried to follow his explanations I couldn't really keep up with him. He even had a slide rule in his pocket and made some calculations, tried to show me what he'd done: "It's a marvelous system, like a huge equation the schedulers are solving all the time."

My father was leaving for Columbus, Ohio, where he had what he called "business opportunities," which is just about all he said about his various pursuits of the American Dream.
"This is going to be *big*," he said, "I'm sure of it. I'll establish myself in Ohio and then you and your sister can come visit."

My shabby, unshaven father hanging out of the train window, holding his felt hat on with one hand, waving with the other, his train leaving right on time.

Just a little bit obsessive

but nothing you have to worry about
just a little bit obsessive
but I don't need a shrink to check me out
just a little bit obsessive
no pills for what I've got
or lots of pills
just a little bit obsessive
don't put me on the No Fly list
just a little bit obsessive
but apart from that I'm just like you
just a little bit obsessive
but aren't we all about things we love
just a little bit obsessive
but it's good to be *obsessive* about something, isn't it
just a little bit obsessive
the way I tell you things
ten thousand times
but I've got to be sure you understand
just a little bit obsessive
about being just a bit obsessive
but if I'm not obsessive
how will I get anything done in this world,

how will I write this letter to you at 4 a.m.
when the whole world's in between
getting up early
and staying up late.

Late

"No, no, don't be sorry," I say,
"don't be sorry. You did what you thought
was best—nothing wrong with that."

I'm still in love with you, or maybe
I'm in love with who we were together,
thirty years ago, on a beach with cloudy weather,
as close as we'd ever be, before you went home
and met and married a good man, Tom,
who gave you the life you wanted, didn't he?

We'd probably have driven each other crazy
but it might have been worth it, who knows?
You're going away tomorrow, I don't suppose
I'll see you again, life's like that—
there's a little joy and the rest of it hurts.

My death

I died on Route 19, got hit by a drunk driver
just at a moment in my life when things were looking up for me:
I'd been promoted to Regional Manager of the *Open All Hours*
convenience stores, and after a lot of lonely years after divorce,
I'd met someone nice, Jackie, a nurse with an autistic son.

We met at a Keep-Fit class and joined a running group, trained
for a 10K together and we were planning to run a half marathon in
March but I was hit by a drunk driver so that was that. (No refund
for my half marathon registration).

What I didn't realize—what most people don't realize—is how the
dead, so-called, are all around us, crowded into rooms that might
seem empty, filling parks and promenades like it's the Day of the Dead,
drifting up and down, up and down hollow streets,
swirling around all the time, circulating currents of the dead.

I joined them.

I like to sit with Jackie and her son Noah, who knows I'm there, even
says, "Hello, Peter," which freaks his Mom out: "Don't say that,
don't *say* that." I hope she'll understand someday.

We're restless, we dead are, we don't sleep, we keep moving,
spirits flowing, doing the best we can with what's left
to us, regretting, of course, that we didn't make more of our lives.

Leaving

$40 in my pocket for gas
and cigarettes. I slip out of Maria's house
while she's sleeping, she knew I'd do that.
Most mornings she'd seemed surprised to see me:
"You still here, Joe?
Thought you'd have been on the road by now."

Time to go,
I start my car, cold morning, and somehow
I feel like I've done something terribly wrong—
I always feel like this when I'm driving
away, starting off again.
I turn on the radio and a preacher tells me to give my soul
to the Lord or I'll be damned for eternity.

Dark road to the highway, rain
beating against the windshield and why is it
that I've always got to leave at 4 a.m.?

Brian Daldorph

Rebecca Wheatley

Still early

I've have used up all my calories on a
Packet of chocolate Hobnobs
3 Babybels and a sausage roll.
I have used up all my patience on
The old man driving his car so slow.
I have given away all my smiling
To the people on the bus I didn't know
as we sat together steaming in our rain drenched clothes.
I have thrown away in winks and wanting
My energy on climbing hills
I was not meant to climb,
Bodies I was not meant to exhume.
I have lived out my expectations
And wasted my years growing into myself.
It's still early and so much is lost.

K.D. Zwierz

Lambs

I saw the carved monks crumbling
and the last few ghosts
of pilgrims
sinking like crumbs into wine,

the shepherd having dusted his hands
of them. Silence on silence
and a setting sun to winter
empty kingdoms.

The cemetery has quietly spread
into the orchard, and the fruit,
softening on the bough and spoiling
in the mud, nourishes only the dead.

The sanctified font stales,
the mould makes it hard to stop
and pray at the water's edge
when the air about's unhallowed.

A farmer speaks a lonely sermon,
a sheep bleats in the cassocked shadows
that finger through the lychgate,
a single lamb lost in the night.

Michael G. O'Connell

The Holiday Joke

Christmas, Hanukkah,
And Kwanza went in the bar.
And all got Blitzened.

Eldritch Carols

From up on the roof
Eldritch carols droning on.
Tentacled horror.

Gary Beck

Historical Reminder

In 341 B.C.
Pericles of Athens
made a funeral oration
to commemorate the dead
in the first year of the war
between Sparta and Athens.
He spoke about the value
of democracy, asserting
'happiness depends on being free'.

Athens was divided
between peace and war,
differing factions,
one for democracy
the other for tyrants.
Their system was imperfect
as are all human endeavors,
yet they didn't violently oppose
contrary beliefs,
but settled them in assembly.

I think about their achievement,
rule of the people
in a time of kings,
a gift to mankind
that took millennia
to appear again
and compare it to my land,
implacably divided
in a complex society
with so many issues
that the only way to survive
will be to learn to get along.

Perhaps our schools
could teach our youngsters
a few lessons from the past
including Pericles who said,
'We are free and tolerant
in our private lives,

but in public affairs
we obey the law'.
Few of our elders
work for the public good
and they will not change,
so it's up to youth
to preserve our future,
before it's too late.

Gary Beck

Dora Rollins

I smell the smog from Lucifer's cigarette

there's a tinge of green
not envy but mold
dust on a forgotten peach
its rinsed skin
beneath my nails
like a silent grenade.

Michael Shoemaker

Inflation Can Kill

Desolation guided desperation
with a silken cord to destruction.
Córdoba, Argentina,
    1989
       monthly inflation
            194%
Grocers put no prices on goods.
They knew while people shopped
the worth of what was in their
baskets evaporated into thin air
as if by one stroke of a
maniacal magician's wand.
Shopkeepers closed their stores
and locked their doors which had
iron bars on the windows.
Food could not be bought at any price.
My missionary companion and I stayed alive
because of one gentle giant of a man
who would open his kiosco en la casa
local shop in his home
under the dead of night so we could buy food
and stuff as much of it as we could into backpacks
and quietly carry it away on bicycles with wheels
that creaked so loud down empty dark city streets.

One day, my missionary companion and I saw
from a bluff overlooking the city
a group of a hundred people or so
from all walks of life heading somewhere.
I asked a man I trusted what they were doing.
He smashed his used-up cigarette nonchalantly
under his boot and said that they were going
to loot that store, pointing his finger north.
I asked what will happen if the police try
to stop them. He shrugged,
but the three of us knew the ticking final answer,
the cold hard math.

Joan E. Cashin

The Ectomorph Has Insomnia

As he tossed and turned, side by side by side
by side by side by side--all six sides,
he thought, I should be able to overcome insomnia.
After all, I have conquered solar systems.
Perhaps travel will help me sleep.

He decided to visit another planet with iridescent lagoons.
When he arrived, he stuck one of his toes in the water,
which turned his blue scales to a new shade of green.
A marvelous fragrance, something that Earthlings would compare to gardenias, came
wafting off the water.
(He had visited Earth hundreds of times.)
It was soothing, but it did not help him sleep.

So he visited another planet, this one covered with craters
from an interplanetary war many centuries ago.
Small golden flowers had sprung up in the craters,
thousands of them, and when the breezes blew,
soft music arose from the little petals. Something that Earthlings would compare to
a harp,
but it did not help him sleep.

He tried another planet, revered for its enormous oceans
which covered the landscape, dwarfing the land mass,
and its purple tides which shifted with every moon.
When he saw her on a beach, all six of his hearts began beating wildly, and he could
not breathe.
This is what Earthlings call love at first sight,
which he knew to be rare, so he proposed. But she refused, saying she would be
exiled if she married an Ectomorph.

Come into exile with me, he pleaded, but she refused again.
So he went to his home planet and wept for a hundred years.
Then, at last, he fell asleep. He dreamed of her,
and only of her. When he woke up, he returned to her planet,
but she was married to someone else.
I will find love again, he declared.
After all, I overcame insomnia.

Alexander Etheridge

Mandala

I dreamt of aspen trees on the moon,
wind from the stars in their crowns.
In the dream I lived
for six thousand years,
listening to the leaves rustle.

I carry my dreams into this world,
even the ones I forget—
As my death creeps closer,
my nightmind respells who I am,
who I'll be in the distances

of eternity—though it may be only
silence. I take the world
into my dreams—everything I lose,
leaf by leaf, shadow after shadow,
each of my collapsing cells

on the dark road towards
a secret, the final unspoken story.
I heard it said that forever is
a pinpoint in the mandala
of infinity, where everything glows.

Kevin MacAlan

Swing

When first that wish gained dreadful traction,
I imagined, where once there was you,
freedom would fill the space about me.
Freedom: the power of liberty.

Aye, I'm free. Free to haunt the night, sleep
at dawn and wake to stare at dishes,
all mine, in a sink of stale soapsuds.
Alone with my art is just alone.

There's only me to judge or pardon.
A son I'll never see shine. Our girl,
the like of you, vernal at your side.
A rusted swing on my unkempt lawn.

Scarcely

Where would euphoria hide
in this feeling of stealing
a tenth of ourselves for us?

In the East they say pleasures,
like mushrooms, have no flower,
have no root, rise anywhere.

In the West we want mushrooms
grown commercially. Force fed
and cultured. Then snatched at death.

What is it we wait for? What
reward hurries us on through
this field of untethered treats?

Gordon Scapens

I'm no refuge

Life soured
by hasty loves,
your view of me
is framed by
what you missed.

Spot me if you can
but I'm buried
under excuses
walking over me
in worn out shoes.

Am I genuine?
I'm as real as you
but we're just failures
travelling a dead end
in search of illusions.

So we've spent time
prancing with each other
from a trampoline
of second-hand prayers
through hoops of lies.

But you don't know me,
you haven't seen the face
behind the face,
you've only been
to the preview.

I am in truth
only a moment
of awareness
ready to howl.

Step by step to…

Keep very still and quiet.
Listen intently for the voice
that will break the monotony.

You will be given a strategy
encouraging action on your part
and a speech of your purpose.

You will be allowed only
a few moments for thought
and then you must act.

Say nothing until your cue,
you'll be given the moment,
and then press one.

You'll speak to one of our staff
who will advise you
you are wasting your time.

Gordon Scapens

Danny D. Ford

North Street Social
for Paul Sims

the wind has turned
gone off fresh
the clouds have lost
the war, but won
the battle & I think
of the woman
you put
on that canvas
in your living room
the one wearing
a blue blazer
& how I said
she looks like
a social worker

& after I polished off
Singapore chow mein
& pissed luminous piss
in your bog
I thought about
my mother's career

I thought about being back home
& I thought about all her old colleagues
the one married to an MP
the one who took
a can of baked beans
to the back
of the head

& I realized why
my mind
had so easily gone there

stern faces
authoritarian
on the job
for you

in the community
wearing respectable blue

you stood her next to
a dried out rotting corpse
and I liked that too

I opened the last can
& listened as you read
your poetry
under a black
Bristol sky.

Lunch at the Dry River after Buco Del Castello

that day
we were wearing
matching hats
& after I gave
directions
the three lads
turned
& laughed
& they
could've been laughing
at my accent
or
at something else
altogether

but I look at us
in matching fucking hats
& I laugh

so I hope
it was that.

Danny D. Ford

Christopher T. Dabrowski

Translated by: Julia Mraczny

Higher Degree of Deconcentration

In the overstimulation age, creativity is not something simple as it was years ago, especially in hard times.

You barely sprout a plot idea, and it's already torpedoed by thought-reminders with a to-do list.

And you'd even turn on the thought-reminder shield if it weren't for the urgencies. Absent-minded thoughts pop up on weekends. You dash off to check social media to see what your friends do, or can't contain your curiosity and turn on your favourite TV series to wake up after a few episodes to realise that a brilliant thought wandered off to someone with a keener eye.

The real nature of Mr X

Five years ago, he fervently adhered to the rules set by his worst enemy.

A few months ago, he became a vegan but still wears leather shoes.

As if that wasn't enough, he professes to be an environmentalist, but he is reluctant to sort his rubbish and prefers to drive a petrol car to an electric one.

After church, he often pops into a friendly VIP brothel, then comes home and lies to his wife, claiming the worked hard and his head hurts.

It makes me sick to see his scabrous mouth.

What is his profession?

He is a politician.

Scott H. Urban

Island

Dan's Dry Cleaning has been closed for hours.
Its parking lot is empty, except for
a Ford Focus from the last century,
one tail light held in place by duct tape.

The driver's door is open, so the couple
can be seen in the roof light's jaundiced glow.
It's clear they're trying to solve a riddle:
how to make the rent, or *how to put*
gas in the tank, or *when to pick up the baby*, or
where to steal the scratch for their next bump.

They sit facing forward, passing back and forth
what might be their last cigarette,
a thin, smoldering communion wafer.
She pushes a strand of hair behind her ear.
He grips the steering wheel as if trying to strangle it.

Neither has heard of John Donne or *Meditation XVII*.
Even if they had, they would say, "John Donne can go fuck himself."

They are adrift; the pair a tiny island unattached to any land.
They cannot see the shore, and they are so far out
no one knows to send a patrol boat to rescue them.

Doraleen

stands at the screen door
off the back of the kitchen
her eyes fixed
in the hundred-yard stare
that takes her gaze
across the stubbly, untilled fields
to the edge of the scrub woods

where that one
patch of fog
hangs suspended
like a ghost with a comfy haunt
even in the height of summer

so familiar
she uses his name when
she murmurs to it

john-roy, i wish you were here
to keep up after it
because i just can't do it
by myself anymore

in our day
we would've called
on the in-laws
for help

but this generation
can't even be bothered
to take a vow;

these girls content
with a fat belly and 'baby-daddy'

cigarette
held between two fingers
turns into a cylinder of ash
like a twig in a forest fire

grandkids
shout from the front room

shut the door, nana;
you're letting out
all the cool air.

Scott Urban

Michael Lee Johnson

Summer is dying

Outside, summer is dying into fall,
and blue daddy petunias sprout ears—
hear the beginning of night chills.
In their yellow window box,
they cuddle up and fear death together.
The balcony sliding door
is poorly insulated, and a cold draft
creeps into all the spare rooms.

Bowl of black petunias

If you must leave me, please
leave me for something special,
like a beautiful bowl of black petunias—
for when the memories leak
and cracks appear
and old memories fade,
flowers rebuff bloom,
sidewalks fester weeds
and we both lie down
separately from each other
for the very last time.

Cathleen Cohen

Painting in Winter

I careen through the market,
forage through aisles and shelves,
grab flowers and fruit to inspire

my students, who will sit for hours
in the dim box of the studio,
mostly in shadow.

Last summer we painted in green
among the linear buzz of mosquitoes,
swifts swooping in wind.

Now it's December. I gather
hothouse squash and nectarines,
whose waxed skin will shine only if spotlit.

Arranged among thrift store scarves,
they might suggest breasts,
lovers, meandering riverbeds, planets.

I want to share secrets, like sketching
before you commit
to larger works and costly pigments.

One of my teachers always painted first
in air. Raising his arms
as if conducting an ensemble,

he wouldn't speak, just sway
as if in a waltz or tango,
no matter what lay before him –

still life or model.
Long, exquisite moments
before touching his brush to canvas.

What should I offer,
painting in air?
Yes. Because it's praise

and how long will things last
in this mute light?

Suzanne Kelsey

Don't forget

when your memories are lost
you are without yourself

the last word
last thing
last
time [is gone]

you are alone

abandoned
by your heart
forgotten
by yourself.

John Grey

Happy Hour

How many times, she wonders,
can she say "No" to the man

before he stops hearing "Yes."
She's alone in a bar.

She tells herself,
"Why shouldn't I be."

She relaxing after a tough day
at the office.

"Isn't that what men do?"
No women are hitting

on the happy-hour guys,
the ones with ties jerked loose

and their top buttons undone.
No women are asking,

"Are you alone?
Do you want company?"

She has a husband at home
just like some of them have wives.

Right now, she's in between
the high pressure of the office

and the low…but still pressure…
of living with someone.

She longs to tell the guy,
"Get lost will you."

But she's lost.
And, for one drink,

maybe two,
it's a good place.

Josh leaves town

I'm leaving town.
No way
they're burying me
in that cemetery
on Potter's Hill.

So long family.
So long Main Street.
So long job stacking shelves
in the hardware store.
So long Friday night football.
So long all the guys and girls
I know from high school.

There's plenty of room
on Potter's Hill
for more coffins.
Even after everyone
I grew up with
is six feet under,
there'll be a plot ready for me.

But excuse me
if I decline the offer.
Who wants to be buried
a half a mile from
where they were born?
What would that say about me?
        "Sure, I remember the guy.
        His life's journey was a half a mile."

So I'm leaving town.
I'm a mile down the road already.
That's twice as long
as some people live.

Your fighter

He's you
but without the black eye,
the broken nose,
the missing teeth.

He's your proxy in the ring.
He's how you hand out punishment,
how you take the blows.

You look like you're in his corner
wielding a sponge
but those are your uppercuts,
your jabs,
your knockout blows.

And yes,
that's your head blown backward
by a glove to the jaw,
your knees buckling,
your body wobbling for a moment
before thumping onto the canvas.

10-9-8..
the referee is counting you out.
Then he's lifting your opponent's arm
as two men and a stretcher
come for your body.

But, as the loser
passes by in semi-consciousness,
you take that sponge
and rub it gently across his cheeks.

A transference occurs.
He's no longer you,
just some bum
who never would listen.

Luckily, you have others in your gym.
There'll be more opportunities for you
to make the substitution.

How I got to be me

I roamed the world
when I was young
and had wonderful adventures.

But then I was told I had to come home,
settle down,
learn something.
My parents started it
but eventually I was the one
who was doing all the telling.

And I obeyed.
Maybe I was weary of
wrestling lions,
tangling with cannibals,
discovering lost cities.
Maybe they were too big
a distraction from mathematics.

Good things came of my decision.
I was able to hold down a job,
fall in love with a wonderful woman,
marry, buy a home,
live happily ever after.

Certainly, the lions thanked me for it.
And the cannibals didn't complain.
And even the cities,
fabulous as they were,
were happy to stay lost.

Did I say 'happily ever after?'
What I meant was
doing my best with what life dealt me.

'Happily ever after'
ended years ago.

Altar piece

since love and marriage
went their separate ways,
you crack eggs in a pan,
burn the toast,
shudder your eyes as you scrape
the blackness from the brown -

breakfast returns to your formidable face,
the dusk of beauty despite it being sunrise -

you shuffle back and forth
with plates and utensils,
no more visions, just an apron,
a husband and two children
long lost to gratitude,
living in your world for lack of anywhere else —

he's off to work,
slipping from the house
like an eel from its coral hole
while two boys
are propelled toward the school bus
by the banging of the front door -

you stand steady
in the resultant silence,
in a sunlit kitchen
that's more like a cathedral portal —

only where is the altar?

not the rusty brown stove
nor the humming white refrigerator —

yet there's stains on your blouse —

the blood and the body
of someone.

Downtown heartache

Nothing worse than a sudden pain
in the region of the heart
when I'm negotiating a crowded thoroughfare.

From being just one of many,
I'm suddenly the sickest person here,
and my impassive face is under threat.

But, within moments, that aching stops,
my anguish retreats, my normal expression
no longer has to cover for me.

Someone else on this street
can now take the lead in human suffering,
a fellow brave man of silence,

and, to think,
he doesn't even know you.

John Grey

Charlotte Amelia Poe

(like daylight)

if i fix all the broken things,
clip my nails
and make good the mess,
will you come back,
in mourning jacket with patched elbows
sun dashed skin and gold whiskey eyes,
drink you in and get heady with it –
can i earn it back?
can i earn it back?
can i earn it back?
can i earn it back?
every second glance,
every brush of fingers,
every stolen smile –
can i earn it back?
can i earn it back?
can i earn it back?
can i earn it back?
the way you said i love you in between lightning strikes –
and thunder rumbles
if i love the ruined things,
will you come back,
and paint the cracks of me pure gold?
(like daylight)

Jim Bates

Exploding Dawn

The sky seemed to suddenly explode at dawn
As the sun rose into a blood red blaze
The clouds were on fire and seemed to be burning
A spectacle unreal that riveted one's gaze
But in the blink of an eye it soon went away
Leaving a memory behind that smoldered throughout the day.

Winter Solstice

During this time of the winter solstice
Gazing up toward the sky at night
Basking a while in celestial splendor
Under stars and constellations bright
And in the infinite universe out there is found
A joyful reverence far from this earthly ground.

William Ross

Lost Ones

Another ice-borne sunrise, the homeless
on the move. Laundromats are locked
and competition for a few heating vents
sends waves of drifters against these
storefronts, unobstructed sunlight a blessing
that holds them.

A few have clung here the winter, limpets in
rude clothing. No one cared to pry them when
the street was an icy shoreline, but now
the afternoons are warm and sewers drink
run-off from the melt.

The lost ones know the signs; the clouds
are angry, ozone warns of gathering rain.
They feel it on their wind-burned
cheeks, hear it in the sudden gust:

You smell and you're bad for business.
No one wants to see you here on the street.

Street Dance

The dance takes place outdoors
in winter weather, music wheezing
from the street.

A threadbare bojangles, one arm
extended, nods to every likely
partner, but they drift away.

The dance goes on too long—
the sun is sky-diving,
the wind grows teeth.

A jingle of coins, the take-out cup
his tambourine, he rings
a song of emptiness,

the cup shakes of its own accord,
a coffee with three sugars
the last warm thing yesterday.

William Ross

Steve Denehan

The First Of September

Summer has stretched
into autumn

the garden is dense
with sunlight and birdsong

a small, very delicate feather
hangs, by a cobweb strand
from a branch
of the sally tree
it moves, but barely

my hands
are not my hands
they are those
of a middle-aged man
I hold them out before me
palms up
as though in offertory
or waiting to receive

the sky is blue and without clouds
the sun is pure, and it is warm, and it is here
that I sit
trying
not to disappear.

That That

Today, my mother told me
that
as a child
I did not like
to be told
what to do

on the drive home
I realised
that that
has always been
the difference
between us.

Steve Denehan

FICTION

LB Sedlacek

Road Etiquette

1) Stop at all checkpoints

Mercury Huffman liked traveling the highways at twilight. He'd stick his thumb out, but no one could see it. They could see him in his black leather jacket, red and blue bandana with white stars covering up what was left of his ponytail long brown hair that had somehow gone gray. His jeans were faded, had holes at the knees, fit snug at the waist, legs and butt. His bag was army green. He'd found it at a surplus store, doubted it had ever seen any kind of action other than to be tagged, scanned and sold to him.

The bag was probably ten years old, acquired after his girlfriend had faded away dying from some kind of hemorrhage. They hadn't dated long hooking up after a friend of his from the road had dated her and then set them up. She'd lived on the coast, outside of Charleston somewhere back up near the swamps and he'd only seen her when he'd be passing through usually between Florida and North Carolina peddling whatever he could carry, whatever he could sell without getting caught.

This time his bag was light, he couldn't risk getting stopped by anyone even for hitch hiking. He was on his way to Savannah to see his sister before she was gone, up to heaven maybe, possibly meeting up with his old girlfriend or whatever.

2)   Pull over for logging trucks

He was almost to Gaffney, South Carolina before he found a ride with an eighteen wheeler up at a truck stop off the interstate. He'd poured in fifty cents twice to take a shower in the men's room then bought a burger with the works, no onions and a cup of coffee. He'd asked around about eight or nine times before he found one going all the way to Georgia. This one wasn't going all the way to Savannah but it would get him further faster than his feet. The trucker had told him to finish his lunch and meet him over at the truck with the royal blue cab with the logo ForTuNeUp. Guy had said he hauled auto parts.

Mercury stood outside the cab, kicked his boots in the dirt wishing he'd had looked for some better walking shoes, had had the cowboy boots since Texas or Arizona he couldn't remember which. The heels had been new then, no scuff marks on any of the leather, and they smelled good too.

"You ready? What'd you say your name was?"

"Mercury. But you can call me Merc. Most folks do."

The driver thrust out a hand. It was thick and wide like he was. He looked mean but his voice was thin and syrupy, soft and he had an accent much like Mercury's but not as pronounced, not as southern. "Name's Pete. Pete Milloway."

"Nice to meet ya, Pete. I appreciate the lift."

"Yeah? Well hop on in."

3) *Follow at a distance*

They sat in silence for a while Mercury letting the glint and glare of the highway soak up over him like a warm bath or a cool shower. Pete would get on the CB every so often and talk to his buddies using abbreviations none of which Mercury knew what they were except for 10-4. Outside of Spartanburg, Pete put down his CB and sputtered a couple of words.

"What'd you say, Pete? Didn't quite make that out."

"Huh? Oh, sorry. I'm not used to having anyone in the cab to talk to."

"Yep. Know the feeling."

Mercury nodded. Scratched his chin. Stared out the windshield some more. The light was fading and sunset was creeping into darkness.

"You wanna grab a bite? Truck stop I usually take is just up over the crest a few miles. I bet you're hungry by now. I'm starving."

Mercury nodded again. Reached into his pocket. Pulled out a wad of small bills. "Sure. Sounds like a good idea. My treat. I got enough for both of us."

Pete shook his head. "Nah. You don't have to do that."

Mercury shrugged his shoulders. "Yeah? You've given me a ride and all. I don't mind."

Pete shifted gears and started slowing down. "Where you from anyway, Merc? You sound like the rest of us around here, but you don't act like you're from the south."

"Me? Yeah, you're right. I'm not from the south. Been here since I was eight. Raised here. I'm originally from Hollister, California. It's one of the three cities that claim the title of earthquake capital of the world if you can believe that. That's all I know about it. I haven't been back since my Daddy packed us up and moved us to Arkansas."

"Eastern southern accent. Yep. Thought I recognized that."

4) *Don't pass a logger*

Halfway through their apple pie, Pete had told Merc pretty much everything there was to know about him. He was the oldest of three kids. Parents were divorced. Lived somewhere in Oklahoma. Finally sold the family house after the kids were grown. They'd had an unusual divorce arrangement living almost next door to each other so it'd be easier on the kids. Pete had two sisters. One was adopted. Mother was part Cherokee or something. Youngest girl had two kids, lived with the father of one of them but he wasn't sure which one. When she turned eighteen the middle girl had gone off to find her real parents but came back after meeting them, not unusual from what he'd heard about adopted kids.

Merc shared some, too. He was the youngest of two kids. He was on his way to see his sister. His father had left them when he was only two so he didn't remember him and didn't much care that he didn't have any memories of him. His mom was in a nursing home in upstate New York, she was from there originally and her sister, his aunt, had thought it was a good idea at the time.

Their plates scraped bare, the family histories traded, the coffee cool, the café long empty, Pete nodded to the bathrooms then back at the truck.

5) *Take your turn on bridges*

It is technically legal to hitchhike from the shoulder of a road or an on or off ramp, whatever you want to call it, if no sign is posted saying that pedestrians are prohibited. But on the highways, it is illegal to hitchhike on the shoulder and near the entrances to these highways unless the hitchhiker stands outside of the highway property.

You can stand at the shoulder's far edge along the highway or at an on ramp or off ramp, take your pick, in an area where there are no local city ordinances that bar hitchhiking. All of this depends, of course, on the state you're in, physically and possibly mentally.

6) *Respect the landowner's rules*

He felt Pete shaking his shoulder and the truck gliding to a stop somewhere close to midnight. He didn't wear a watch but he figured they'd been on the road that long crossing the Georgia state line after dark. "This is the end of the line for me, Merc. Thanks for the company."

Merc watched him drive off resisting the urge to throw out his thumb the minute he was out of sight of Pete's rearview window. He started walking kicking up dust with his boots. He wasn't sure how far he was from Savannah but he thought Pete had said something about it being around thirty miles or so to the city limits. He was too close to chance it and walking in the night air felt good with the scents and the quiet. He wasn't tired, had slept some in the truck in-between country tunes and Pete's CB conversations. He was a little hungry, the pie and meal at the diner was starting to wear off. He figured there might be a rest area up ahead and usually there were vending machines with crackers and sodas, enough to keep his tummy busy for awhile.

7) *Drive a vehicle in excellent condition*

Janel had been sick for some time, that's what her doctor was telling him and he'd figured the same the few times he'd been able to call and ask how she was doing. Janel's doctor was a square shape with rimless glasses, a scruffy beard, peppery white hair. He bent over her now. Janel's husband had taken off years ago, come back, taken off again; come back and finally came to his end from some sort of heart condition. Janel's illness had managed to avoid that organ but she had it far worse, a kind of cancer in the liver or somewhere close. The medical terms had started running together after he realized that he had a better chance of seeing Pete next week than he did his sister.

8) You may have to sign a register, and/or pay an access fee

The view was the same. The same as he remembered it from the back porch, white, paint peeling, boards creaking as you walked on them. It was silent. Janel was asleep in the back bedroom. He couldn't hear anything from the neighbors. The river was silent too gurgling along shuffling brown mud, bugs and other water critters through the lazy water. He didn't remember how long Janel had lived in the house. It was one story with a front and back porch, everything white or used to be white with dinginess or peeling paint replacing the solid strong color in certain spots. The ground was flat, greenest by the riverbanks, dull brown by the house. He sat back and sighed, slung some lemonade down his throat letting out an "ahh" of sorts the only sound within three or four miles he guessed. He liked the end to the silence so he said "ahh" again and took another sip of lemonade wondering if he had enough to finish out the day and even the evening.

9)   Logging roads often take their half of the road out of the middle

Janel hadn't lasted much past the night he'd sat out on the porch sipping lemonade. He remembered the cold drink, the color a bright pink and that it was just sitting there in the refrigerator. He had poured himself a glass then another and then another until it was empty and he hadn't wondered who'd made it or how it got there but just that it was there and it was good and cold and kept him busy instead of thinking about Janel. She was his only sibling, younger too and no kids. He didn't bother to try and reach the ex's kin if any of them were still around. Janel had told him about looking her ex up on the internet once and how she'd found out he started some kind of group dedicated to not making alimony payments. She had laughed when she told him about it saying that the SOB had never paid her the first dime in alimony so what was he complaining about. He had liked that about Janel. She told it to you straight; he was always saying and had said the very same thing at the service. There was no flash with Janel, but she was kind, decent and hard working and she'd even tried the settling down thing even though it didn't work out so good for her. She at least had given it a shot.

10) Truck wheels can fling rocks with such force that they damage windshields or kick up so much dust that you can't see

There wasn't much left to clean up. Some old shoe boxes under the bed stuffed with the usual photos, recipes, what anyone might expect to find in an unguarded cardboard safe of sorts that anyone could find, open, take. Mercury had fished out some photos from one of the boxes, pulled some socks out of the ex's dresser that he thought would fit. That's what he needed the most on the road, Janel would always ask and that's what he always told her and at his birthday or close enough to it somehow a new bundle of socks would wind up wherever he was or somewhere nearby so that he could get them. He'd always kid her and ask her how she knew where to find him and she would simply smile and never answer.

11) Logging roads are on private lands and driving on them is a privilege not a right

There was no one else on the road at this hour, the air cool and crisp on his face and just the right amount so he wasn't too cool or too hot. He had hoofed it maybe a mile or two already out of Savannah. There wasn't anything to keep him there, her home Janel had left to him but he'd signed all the right papers and the lawyer doing all the arrangements promised to wire him some cash when he needed it when he was in one place again. He'd given him some hundreds and Mercury had pushed the cash back saying I don't need it but the lawyer – a guy Janel had told him she liked – shoved it right back. He shrugged his shoulders and took it. He'd also tried handing him a cell phone but he'd refused wishing now that he hadn't so he could call someone or maybe get the weather or the time. Janel was his last link to a plan and he never had one, but now he thought maybe he should find something or some place and stick to it. Janel would agree, he knew it.

12) Carry plenty of fuel because most roads have limited or no services available

When he got in one place, the lawyer did as he said and wired him some money. The place was by a lake. Lake Russell.

There were no homes along the shoreline of Lake Russell. It was undeveloped, lots of untouched scenery and fishing. He would have to learn how to fish, maybe forage, scrounge for grubs. He'd set up the tent he'd gotten at a trading store just outside the lake.

It was bright blue and reminded him of a picture that had hung in the stairwell just outside of Janel's room, her room in their childhood home. The picture was also a lake but in colors not normal for lakes, a pink, a red, possibly some green he couldn't remember all of them.

He had spent a lot of time looking at that picture and wondering who lived there at that pink and red lake and what they did there and were they any more settled than he was. It was just a picture, but it seemed real to him just like Janel, just like Pete Milloway, and just like the pink lemonade.

LB Sedlacek

Terry Sanville

Harley and Pawla

Harley raised his head and listened, his tail flicking from side to side. Most of the others sat on their haunches and stared upward.

"They feed us scraps twice a week. That's ridiculous," he muttered.

"Tell me about it," Sharon said from the adjacent cell, stopping her incessant licking for just a moment. "Then they release us into the arena and think we'll be grateful for eating a few scrawny Christians and convicts. I'm so tired of how they taste, and you gotta eat at least two to feel full."

"Yeah, for me they're like potato chips," Gladys said, smirking. "You can't eat just one."

The rest of the females in her cell stared at Harley and hissed, knowing he'd get the lion's share of any food dumped from above.

Harley yawned, showing long yellowed fangs. "Yeah, well eating Christians is better than starving – or worse, getting attacked by those idiots with spears. None of us lives through those fights."

"You should complain to our union rep," Sharon said.

Harley snorted. "Which one? They change every week."

"Yeah, I've noticed. That contract we pawed in Africa was soooo bogus. The sex workers in Algiers have better contracts than we do. I knew I should've run like hell. But they were rounding up whole prides and I thought, ya know, maybe a vacation in the City would be good."

"You're such a numbskull, Sharon. We're all gonna end up bones in the ground along with the gladiators, venatores, Christians and convicts. And the death benefits from the union won't pay diddly squat."

As the food dropped through the hatches from above, fights broke out among the females. The Romans kept the males in separate cells and Harley had one to himself, being such a badass and a hungry one. After eating what little the jailers gave him, he stretched out on the floor of his cell, its straw marked by piles of poop. The quarters stank worse than elephant dung. He longed for the open plains, the whistle of the afternoon wind, the heat from the sun warming his fur. Death might be a blessing. The Christians had it easy.

Just before darkness closed in, the jailers brought in a caged beast and released it into the cell next to his.

"Oh great," Margret said, growling. "Now we gotta put up with her. Less food for the rest of us."

The tigress paced her cell, muttering insults under her breath. "You think I like being stuck in this hellhole with you freakazoids?"

"Hey, I kinda like her stripes and those cute little ears," Harley said. "What's your name, honey?"

"Up yours, buddy. Try anything and I'll give you a good swat. And that coat of yours – I've seen dead camels that look better."

Harley sat on his haunches and stared at the new arrival. "Well, you don't have to get nasty. I'm from Africa. Where are you from?"

"Armenia. I was minding my own business, killing a few goats in the hill country up near the big mountains when I got trapped in a pit by the locals and sold to the Romans. They shipped my ass across the Aegean. Got seasick and the sailors just laughed at me. Idiots."

The tigress stopped pacing and approached the bars. She slumped onto the floor, rolled onto her back and stretched. "I'm so damn horny I could growl all night."

"Please don't," Harley said, snickering. "My harem is already pissed and I'm sure jealous. My name's Harley, by the way."

"I'm Pawla. Let's give them something to growl about. Come over near the bars."

Harley rose and collapsed next to the iron bars that separated their cells.

Pawla sniffed his butt then began licking his coat, as much as she could. "Jeez, Harley, when was the last time anybody cleaned you?"

"Doesn't seem that important in this place. Tomorrow, I'm supposed to fight a bull in the arena. I'm not as fast as I used to be and . . ."

"Don't worry about it," Pawla said. Bulls are stupid. All you gotta do is grab them by the neck and it's all over."

"You've done this before?" Harley asked in surprise.

"Back in Armenia, I ate real well, until I got captured."

The big cats lay on their sides, backs to the bars, sharing body heat. Fragments of voices from the pride rumbled through the cells, ". . . a real tramp . . . not even here an hour and . . . you can't trust Harley . . . he'd mate with the jailer if he could . . . can you imagine how ugly their cubs would be . . . she's got more rolls of fat than a pregnant sow. . . bet those fangs of hers are implants . . . I like the stripes, so stylish – but try getting a matching shoulder bag that color."

The following day Harley returned from the Colosseum's arena, exhausted but largely unscathed. Pawla's cell stood empty and he figured he'd never see her again. The Romans had pitted her against a massive bear from the Atlas Mountains, a fierce beast difficult to bring down. But eventually she returned with only one claw mark on her magnificent coat. The two cats shared stories with much grumbling from the pride. Harley licked her wound, which didn't look serious and they fell asleep, side-by-side.

The days and weeks passed. The Romans pitted both of the big cats against an assortment of animals: gazelles, antelopes, jackals, ostriches, hyenas, wild boar, bears, bulls, and even elephants. Sometimes Harley killed alone, sometimes as part of the pride, and a few times with Pawla. The two worked well together, much to the disgust of his own kind. Rumors abounded that the pride might turn on Harley if he kept up his illicit relationship with Pawla. But it got even worse.

"I hear you're scheduled to fight the venatores in two days," Pawla said as she paced her cell.

"Yeah, they'll come at me in packs with spears. I'll kill some but they'll get me. I'm done for."

"No you're not. They've scheduled me at the same time. It'll be us against them. I'll have your back."

"Still, there's more of them than we can handle."

The two cats sat licking each others' coats through the bars. Sharon and Gladys looked away in disgust, having no sympathy for the couple's inter-species love. Finally, Pawla stretched out on the straw and Harley did the same, their heads close together.

"Did you see what they're doing to the Colosseum?" Pawla whispered.

"What are you talking about?"

"They're raising the wall around the arena."

"Why?"

"Evidently last week some pissed off panther jumped up into the seats and mauled a concessionaire selling figs and cherries. The cat was killed before she could escape."

"Yeah, but panthers are light and can really fly."

"Hey, lard ass, if you try, I know you can make that jump," Pawla said and yawned. "And I know I can. Made jumps higher than that back in Armenia."

"So what do we do if we make it into the grandstands?"

The couple kept their heads together all that evening and tried to work out the details. Harley would have to abandon any hope of receiving the promised pension from the union and Pawla and her kind were unrepresented – another reason why the lions distrusted her. The following day they went over all the details while the pride glowered.

The jailers came for them right after high sun. Using a slave-powered elevator, they lifed the cats up from below and through a trapdoor into the center of the arena. The Colosseum looked packed with citizens already half drunk on wine from the Chianti region. They screamed for blood. From a portal in the side of the arena six men emerged, wearing white tunics and carrying short spears. They didn't look too eager to confront the cats. The Roman guards had to shove the last one through the opening and slam the door behind him. The crowd roared with laughter.

Pawla and Harley circled the center of the arena and let out the most ferocious roars they could muster. The citizens responded with clapping and cat calls. The spearmen flattened themselves against the wall, their knees shaking. The couple turned to the crowd and pawed the air, fangs bared. More hoots and laughter from the audience. Meanwhile the spearmen peed themselves.

Pawla turned to Harley and murmured. "Are you ready? We'll get only one chance."

"Whoever makes it, just keep going."

"You bet."

The two took several deep breaths then charged the spearmen who stood shoulder to shoulder, weapons thrust before them. Both cats reached top speed and were within feet of the venatores when the men broke ranks and scattered. But the cats kept going and leaped upward toward the grandstands, their momentum throwing them into a row of wide-eyed screaming citizens who scrambled to evade the monsters.

"This way," cried Pawla and the couple dashed out one of the Colosseum's many entrances and into the streets of old Roma. At the edge of town they found a narrow garbage-filled lane between what looked like slave quarters and stank worse than their Colosseum cells. They slunk into the shadows, out of sight from the main strada.

"I think my chest is gonna explode," Harley complained. "I remember why I let the gals do the hunting. All that running would kill me."

"Don't worry, I'll have you on a healthy diet in no time. Only lean meats and exercise for you. No more of those fatty Christians."

"Whatever you say, dear."

Throughout the afternoon they listened to marching cohorts of Roman soldiers brandishing spears, swords and shields, searching the neighborhoods. None dared to venture into their squalid alley. The couple waited until dark then sneaked out Porta Metronia and headed south.

"How far do we have to go?" Harley asked, his one paw sore from trotting along stone-paved streets.

"The Lepini Mountains are two or three days' travel from here. We'll move only at night."

"Yeah, humans can't see jack in the dark. And they're the apex predators? What a joke."

"But they've got the tools and the numbers, and some say the brains."

"Yeah, a lot of good that did those Christians."

The couple traveled stealthily through the nights and slept during the days, out of sight of any roads. They moved into the mountains, found a valley with a small lake and streams and settled into establishing their territory, not hard since there were only a few scrawny panthers within miles and they cleared out quickly once Harley and Pawla showed up.

Harley hated the winter cold while Pawla loved it. They hunted deer, wild boar and goats, and when game grew scarce raided the sheepherders' camps. The few locals complained to the authorities. But nobody believed their stories of big cats, one striped and one with a magnificent mane, prowling the valleys and mountain passes. And the stories got even weirder over the years with sightings of strange-looking cubs with big heads and pale stripes. But the number of livestock taken by these beasts seemed small and as time passed, sightings shifted into the realm of fantasy. Harley's and Pawla's legacy became a fun love story told to children, until it too faded into history.

Terry Sanville

Doug Hawley

Death Row Magazine

"This month's exclusive article is on the final meals for the inmates before they are put to death. We have been to many prisons in several states which have the sense to deprive t the dregs of society, the worthless, and the craven of the right to have any more chances to harm society."

"We are not naming the prisons or the true names of the soon to be deceased. In many cases they have no remorse, or even claim that they do not deserve to be executed. We will not be a party to giving the miscreants any chance to brag or claim injustice."

"Let's meet Bobby X. He is slated to die in a week. He murdered five in a Synagogue, three in a Mosque, and four in a Catholic church in a tri-state rampage. What's on the plate for that special day Bobby?"

"Before I answer that, just let me say that I'm not a bigot, you might even say I'm ecumenical regardless of what the papers say. I'm not forgetting your question. Listen, dammit, I want Coke with the meal. Trying to pass off Pepsi makes me mad enough to kill. Do I get to say that?"

"Sure Bobby."

"The Coke better be Hecho En Mexico. The USA uses a different sugar, and it's not nearly as good. I want the family meal from each of Burger King, MacDonald, and Pizza Hut. I'll nibble a little of each and do a taste test. The warden promised to publish my review, you know, after."

"Is that enough Bobby?"

"Sure, you think I want indigestion?"

"OK, catch you on the other side. Thanks for your time."

"Sure, I have nothing else to do and I enjoyed the company."

"Emily J. killed her three children by deliberately ramming her car into a tree at ninety miles an hour with Joey six, Tory eight, and Jerry eleven. She said that they were all better off dead, and she wished that she had died with them. I want to know a little more about her situation before we get to the meal. What do you say Emily?"

"Since I'm a goner in two days, I might as well fess up. After my third husband and I divorced, my new boyfriend said he didn't want a readymade family. Supposedly leaving the kids without safety seats and disabling their air bags would be sure to kill them while I would survive with minor injuries and be free to marry Jefferson. We were stupid when we thought we were smart and told four people we thought were good friends who could keep a secret. I'm through with those creeps. Then the car got examined and our rigging was caught."

"Well Emily, tough luck. Back to the meal."

"I'd like to try some things that I've never had, something exotic: A peanut butter sandwich with Oreo cookies, a Chardonnay chocolate float, orange slices, and Brazil nuts."

"If you show up in the same place Emily, say hi to Jefferson when you join him."

This is your correspondent Jack Wheeler signing off for this month but be sure to continue the story in the July Death Row Magazine, available by subscription or at your supermarket checkout. You won't believe what that drug-crazed champion bodybuilder is having just before he goes to the electric chair or the mild-mannered actuary before he visits the hangman.

Doug Hawley

Stephen McQuiggan

An Abject Lesson

'I staged a break in,' Parker stood by the whiteboard, addressing the rest of the class, one hand in the lapel of his immaculate, and expensive, blazer, '...at the holiday home, of course. I didn't want the inconvenience of living in squalor at the old primary homestead, you understand.' He gave a mock grimace, and received a smattering of titters in reward, until Mr Gray hushed the room with an icy glance.

'Continue,' said the teacher when the silence prevailed.

'Where was I? Oh yes, the fake burglary – petty theft, broken pane, blah blah blah.'

Mr Gray raised an eyebrow. 'I must say I'm very disappointed in –'

'And then I killed my Father,' Parker interrupted him. 'I beat him to death with one of his own walking sticks. The same one he used to beat me with in fact, which lends a certain poetry to the whole endeavour, don't you think? Hell of a thing ... his brains splattered all over Mother's favourite Persian rug. There's no cleaning that I'm afraid. Still, there's always a price to pay.'

There was an audible gasp in the classroom. Mr Gray steepled his fingers, staring hard at Parker (who exuded a cancerous level of smugness) as if trying to determine his veracity, but Bailey didn't need to look at him to know he was telling the truth – the cocky bastard was many things, but a liar wasn't one of them. It was one of the reasons he was Gray's little pet – besides, such a claim could be easily verified and there was no way Parker would get himself suspended for such a traceable boast.

How Bailey always despised the first day back at school and the awful competition of revealing what assignments you'd completed during the mid-term break.

'You murdered your own Father?' Mr Gray pressed the beaming Parker.

'Yes, Sir, I did. I knew it would be risky but I followed the text books to the letter, especially the chapter on concealment, paying particular attention to Flyte's thesis on misdirection of course. I even defecated on the pantry floor.'

'Ah, the adrenalin deposit of the anxious thief,' Gray nodded, 'a most subtle touch.'

'Thank you, Sir.' Parker flicked off some lint that had the temerity to land on his lapel. 'Anyhoo, long story short, the police have arrested a local vagrant for the crime – their suspicions aroused, no doubt, by the fact that I slipped my Father's wallet in his tatty pocket as he slept in a shop doorway. Mother is taking the whole family on an extended sojourn to Biarritz to recover from the ordeal.'

He nodded to the large manila folder he had left on the teacher's desk. 'You'll find all the details in there – the planning, execution, alibi and whatnot – plus the glossary, of course.'

'Thank you, Parker,' said Mr Gray, tapping the folder with his thin lady fingers, 'I'm confident it will make for some interesting reading. You may return to your seat.'

Parker flowed back to his desk on a wave of unbearable complacency; there was a bulge in his trousers as if, for some purpose known only to himself, he had secreted a Dutch onion down there. Mr Gray's eyes scanned the room and Bailey held his breath.

'Mr Potter,' he said finally, and Bailey sighed in relief, 'would you care to come up and regale us with your mid-term report?'

Potter, with much squeaking of his chair, made it onto his feet, his face already resigned to humiliation. Bailey understood completely – after Parker's revelation, what was the point in this charade? Parker had always been the star student – after his report everyone else's was going to appear like very small beans and, consequently, leave them open to Gray's withering critique.

Potter placed his, very slender, file on the teacher's desk as he passed. He turned to face his classmates, wearing an expression that would not have looked out of place on Job, and fiddled nervously with his tie as he cleared his throat to begin. An air of vacancy enveloped him, like one who had grown used to being perpetually ignored and subsequently retreated into a form of emotional hibernation.

'I – I- I,' he stammered and Parker banged loudly on his desk. Parker *always* banged his desk whenever someone was floundering on their report. Usually they managed to get out a few paragraphs before Parker struck up his raucous tattoo, but it was obvious to everyone, from the first stuttering note, that Potter was in trouble.

'I – I,' he carried on gamely, 'I sent a few n-n-nasty letters to my n-n-neighbour.'

'And?' Gray sighed, and Parker's fists drummed enthusiastically once more.

'And, well, they were, y'know, p-p-poison p-p-pen letters. She lives alone, y'see, and she's quite elderly. I think they might just push her over the edge and –'

'Have you read Stridelle's treatise on malicious correspondence?'

'Um, yeah ... I mean yes, Sir.'

'And can you remind the class of his conclusion?'

'He, um, he said that...'

'He said that,' Gray banged his own desk in imitation of his star pupil, 'it was totally ineffective in the long term! He found such missives to garner sympathy and pity in fact, the total opposite of the effect you were trying to achieve, no?'

'Y-y-yes Sir.'

'Sit down, boy. This is typical of your work – more of the same using less of the brain. Rest assured I will be drafting some exceedingly nasty letters myself tonight and sending them to your sponsor.'

Potter hurried back to his seat and held his twitching head in his hands. He was never going to graduate and what would become of him then? That was a fear we all have to live with, Bailey thought, all of us except for Parker.

Gray ran a finger down his roster once more, a brief smile flickering across his spittle flecked lips. 'Miss Ellis?' he said in a softer tone.

Ellis got up clutching her folder to her chest and Bailey's belly did a little tumble. She was easily the prettiest girl in class, just flawed enough to be perfect, and had been scoring high before the break. She offered her folder to Gray – making him take it rather than just setting it before him, a subtle power-play the teacher acknowledged with a tightening around the eyes – then turned to face her peers.

Bailey had been looking forward to this. It was the only time he had an excuse to gaze at her head on. Her voice had a seductive lilt that made everyone lean forward, even though it was firm enough to be heard at the back of the room. Parker folded his arms – there would be no sarcastic banging of fist on wood during *her* report.

'I got myself a babysitting job over the holiday,' Ellis began, her big green eyes darting here and there, intent on engaging everyone in the room simultaneously. 'I made sure I found myself alone with the father as often as possible – got him to give me a ride home, rubbed up against him going through doorways, bent over a lot to retrieve rattles and dummies, you get the general idea.'

I sure do, Bailey thought, shifting uncomfortably in his seat as other ideas, more nuanced than general, flooded his brain.

'I wore short skirts and low cut tops, played the giggly, dumb bitch and he lapped it up. It was only a matter of time before he made his move. Of course, I made it very clear I was underage, but men only ever believe the make-up. They only see what they want to.'

'And?' Gray butted in.

'Well,' Ellis smiled at him, oh so sweetly. 'One day when Daddy Dearest was out with his wife and I was alone with the brat I stumbled across his laptop.' She mimed opening it up and tapping on the keys. 'Then, using the techniques from week two of the course, I found his password and accessed his files. Then I proceeded to download a prodigious amount, a *frightening* amount, of child porn onto his hard drive.'

There was a murmur of approval amongst the males in the class, even though this was one of their biggest nightmares. Anyone brave enough to date Miss Ellis would have to be extremely careful on how they broke up with her.

'The last few occasions I refused all offers of a ride home, flinched whenever he came close. I engineered it so that his wife found me in tears in the kitchen. I started wearing baggy clothes, no make-up – all standard stuff from Module One, and all designed to make her suspicious. I made ridiculous excuses when she called to book my services. When she asked me what was wrong I told her I'd never babysit for them again and hung up.'

'Was that effective?' Gray enquired.

Bailey stifled a snort – Ellis was a consummate actress (she had came top of the class in simulated crying), in fact during her performance test the tutor had actually brought her out into the corridor to ask if she really was okay.

'Highly,' Ellis nodded. 'I saw her walking to work when normally he drove her. There was obviously a burgeoning estrangement.' She clasped her hands demurely and smiled shyly, every inch the innocent. 'Last week I made a tearful confession of his inappropriate behaviour to my parents who promptly contacted the police. I watched them carry out several items of interest from his house after they arrested him. I doubt it'll come to trial. If I'm any judge of character,' she grinned (she'd aced the character assessment module too), 'there's a very strong chance he'll opt for the easy way out.'

Bailey felt like clapping. It was so clean, so clinical, and so typical of the girl.

'Very efficient,' Gray acknowledged, 'but I can't help feeling it all somehow beneath you.'

'Sexuality is the greatest weapon in a young girl's arsenal, or so you've always taught us.'

'True,' Gray agreed, 'and I applaud the textbook application of your feminine wiles, but that's what also rankles.' He smiled at Ellis as if to soften the blow. 'It's all a bit routine for a girl of your talents. Of course, it's fun to destroy someone with your body, but how much more satisfying to use the mind. You're almost sixteen now – you're window on this type of thing is fast closing – you should be concentrating more on the experimental, the unexpected. A solid report, and a high mark will reflect that, but I can't help but feel a tad disappointed.'

Ellis smiled politely and returned to her seat. Bailey felt so bad for her he didn't have the heart to admire her coltish legs as she sashayed past.

'Now, let's see,' Gray said, scanning the register once more. He glanced up at the class as if searching for inspiration and an inner voice told Bailey his moment had arrived. He stared out the window with a faraway look in his eyes – a sure-fire way to gain the teacher's wrath.

'Mr Bailey,' Gray bellowed, 'perhaps you'd like to share your holiday project with the rest of us – if you can manage to tear yourself away from your daydreams.'

'Certainly, Sir,' Bailey said, wincing a little as Parker struck up a death march on his desktop. *Go easy,* he mentally implored Parker, *at least wait until I've started.* He positioned himself and cleared his throat.

'Haven't you forgotten something?' Gray asked, his index finger pointing to the empty space where Bailey should have left his typed report.

'No, Sir, my report is mainly oral.'

Gray frowned. 'You've been struggling through the majority of the course so far. I hope, for your own sake, you're not going to allow your natural laziness to drag you down. Your sponsors have invested a great deal of money and time in you – they will not be too pleased with *my* report which, I can assure you, will be both comprehensive *and* typed.'

Parker banged on his desk in a flurry of malicious anticipation.

'I think you and my sponsors will both be pleasantly surprised, Sir.'

'Begin then,' Gray huffed, 'though you needn't think you've set a precedent – I have already docked you marks, surprise or no.'

Ellis was staring at him intently. Bailey didn't know if that was because she was willing him on, or because she wanted him to fall flat on his arse and take the bad look off her own report. Either way, he couldn't return her stare. She was too much of a distraction. He turned his gaze onto the conceited, oh so pleased with himself, Parker – that self-satisfied mug was all the incentive he needed.

'I spent most of the term break carrying out research,' he began.

'No, no, no,' Gray interjected, 'You were supposed to have had your research completed in school time. Mid- term is for implementation and –'

'I said *most* of the break,' Bailey bulldozed on. 'I spent the rest implementing it. The reason I had to spend extra time on the research side is because what I was after isn't covered in any of the modules we've done so far. I don't think we're due to study what I needed until our final year, in fact.'

'Sir,' Parker was holding up his hand, 'you clearly stated in the assignment that we had to work from the texts *as taught.* You warned we would be marked down if we tried to improvise from future texts.'

'That's quite correct, Parker. And what do you have to say to that, Mr Bailey?'

'I'd say I did stick to the text, though perhaps I coloured outside the lines a little.'

'If you're going to insist on wasting everyone's time then perhaps you should return to your seat.'

'I haven't finished my report,' Bailey snapped, '*Sir.*' Parker drummed out another quick roll on his desk. 'Once my research was complete I broke into the school.'

There was a sharp, collective intake of breath then a thick void of silence. School property was sacrosanct. It was written into the confidentiality clause.

'A breach of the rules, certainly,' Bailey continued, 'but one I'm sure you'll forgive when you witness the fruit of my labours.'

Gray pondered Bailey for quite some time. 'I'm afraid,' he said, just as Parker struck up his ominous beat once more, 'you leave me with no other option than to expel –'

At the word 'expel', Parker built up to a virtuoso frenzy. There was a dull explosion, a small plume of smoke, and the smell of barbecued flesh. The drumming on the desk had ceased abruptly, for there was no more desk – just the armless torso of Parker seated behind its splintered ruins. Most of his smug skull was draped over his shoulders, or splattered on his nearest classmates. As the shrieks died down Bailey afforded himself a smile.

'I set up a controlled detonator, set to go off when his drumming reached its optimal level. It was a very localised blast, so as to spare my fellow students injury of course. A bang for a bang – I thought it lent a certain poetry to the whole endeavour, don't you think, Sir?'

Bailey returned to his seat and Ellis smiled at him as he sauntered by. He was confident that, with her at least, he'd scored an A*.

Stephen McQuiggan

Gabriel Lukas Quinn

On A Date

with my never-quite-official ex-boyfriend, we found ourselves staggering out of a sweltered Indian restaurant, stomachs full of curry—mine fuller than his. In my sweating right hand, I held a package full of garlicked flatbread, nuisant carbs I insisted he take but knew would end up in my fridge. I didn't want to waste good food, even if it wasn't food good for me.

Why doesn't he understand that?

The sun screamed scarlet, unfiltered, off the Hawthorne shop windows. We paraded down the street in our stealthy little way. I sang the lyrics to a song I didn't really know. Push it. Push it real good. He corrected me: Whip it good. I don't know how I felt, but I laughed it off. He seemed upset, pouted his lip. When we turned a corner, there was a man sitting on a street bench, pressed against a brick wall. He squeezed an empty water bottle that looked just as crystal cold as if it had been full. His face in the sunlight was nothing but ginger scraggle. I slowed, mystified. He asked if I was gonna eat all that. He motioned, with the plastic water bottle, toward the plastic-wrapped flatbread in my sweaty right hand. His life sat piled against the building behind him. Stained. Unfiltered. The breeze that blew down the alley was lively and sweet, some kind of juxtaposition. I glanced at him—my ex, not the streety—waiting, expecting. His lips still pouted. "Yeah, I am. Sorry," I said, now staring at the pile of anonymous personal things, things tossed against the wall. What else could I add? I knew there ought to be more. "Sorry," I added. I didn't look into his eyes. As we walked on, he said something to the back of our heads; it was hurtful in its understanding, its forgiving, its emancipation. I don't remember what it was anymore; I just remember wishing he hadn't said it, wishing he had lashed out, wept, maybe attacked. We were a block away before I spoke again. "I don't know why I did that," I said. I crunched the flatbread in my sweaty right hand. The shop windows on this block were boarded up—some graffitied, condemned. I hoped there might be another vagrant looming around the next alleyway, but there never was. "I think it's my parents' fault," I continued. My ex nodded. When we located my car, we slipped inside. My ex didn't have his own; I drove him most places. It was toasty, sticky, like baking cookies. "Should we go back? See if he's still there?" I turned the key in the ignition. He shrugged. The engine ground its teeth. "Maybe I'll volunteer at a shelter sometime," I said. I pulled out, careful not to clip the Honda behind me. "But I'm busy, y'know?"

He knows.

I dropped him off at the corner of his street, far enough so I was invisible from his house—and his house was invisible to me. He smiled and waved. Now I was the one with the pouty lip. Still, I waved back, his form disappearing. That was our last date; I haven't seen him since. But I've seen many hobos since then—some of them wanted food, some money, some other things I could never discern. I've donated clothes to shelters; I've volunteered at soup kitchens. Nothing works. I still feel the lack gnawing.

What could I possibly give to make it all better? I worry about that a lot. It runs through my head some nights, like unfiltered tap water, invisibly tainted. Sometimes it only drips like a leak. I wish I could turn it off. Then I could sleep well again.

Gabriel Lukas Quinn

Damian Tarnowski

The Middleman

They had all begun arguing and blaming each other. This was not the way things were supposed to be. The heavenly cherubs should not have been raising their voices in thunderous anger and the hellish hounds should not have been roaring with unconditional rapture.

To all intents and purposes, Claude Mombasa had kept the peace since the Second World War doing his job diligently, but something was uncomfortably amiss. Normality had taken a break and was watching the unfolding balls-up whilst enjoying a nice cup of tea and a chocolate hobnob. There was always the odd skirmish when the numbers did not equate but this was getting out of control.

For the forces of good and evil to be happy, alignment was key across the board. Quotas had to be even; otherwise, all heaven, as well as all hell, would break loose. His position was a high-pressure, twenty-four-seven, well let's face it, timewise - an infinite assignment and he had to keep everyone chipper. After all, he was all there was to stop an all-out war between them.

He had been chosen by both sides as the outstanding candidate for the job due to his quiet composure as an emissary in his previous life. He was an experienced navigator around turbulent issues, stopping countless battles with a cool head as everyone around him lost theirs. His skill set was ideal for countering rising conflict and keeping an everlasting peace. He was also reasonably good at counting.

He lived between upstairs and downstairs, overseeing what was known as Purgatory. He preferred to think of it as more of a teaching-cum-arranging-cum-twilight zone and tended to use the acronym T.A.T.Z for short. Originally, he had thought of it as a teaching-cum-integration-cum-twilight zone but had quickly dismissed that idea for fear of offending the W.I. He would have unquestionably been searching for a new career if he had gone down that road as they were possibly only second in power to the deities. Best just to change the acronym.

Purgatory was a grey, drab place created and designed for functionality as opposed to being aesthetically pleasing. As the numbers to be dealt with were colossal, there was an overwhelming need for categorisation. Colossal numbers meant a colossal staff were needed to supervise this process ergo office upon office dominated the domain. Dull, uninspiring but handy if you loved quantitative and secretarial work.

Nothing was set in stone regarding where you initially ended up once you had kicked the bucket. He had to classify those that had been unclassifiable when they were alive as well as attempting to provide a 'last chance saloon' tutelage to individuals deemed lucky enough to be given a second chance. All in all, a fairly hefty workload.

T.A.T.Z was set up by both sides to fix the shocking bureaucratic mismanagement. All the toing and froing with these borderline cases was not doing either side any favours and over countless eons had become somewhat of a bugbear. It was deemed top priority to sort out the wheat from the chaff and put an end to the logistical nightmare. However, the system was still flawed and perhaps due to simple oversights or maybe clerical gaffes from underlings, some always managed to worm through the safety net.

From above, he accepted ill-judged riffraff who poked fun at virtuous innocents as well as provoking distress from radiant devotees, simply for their own selfish gratification. He also welcomed wronged folk from below who were far too happy for their own good, having the cheek to go out of their way to bring the darkness avoidable mirth, light and joy. All came into his throng and had either to be correctly admonished or due to administrative bloopers, sent into the appropriate groups where they should have primarily been.

With those who were listed to be taught the error of their ways, he attempted to guide them by using rather unorthodox methods that he hoped they would take on board. Some learned, others did not.

He recently had two sisters who were killed in a car crash. Their deaths were caused by incessant squabbling; one having a go at the other till they got into fisticuffs and their car careered off the cliff road to their doom. They had regularly fought like cat and dog, so he had joined them at the hip as a Siamese and a Great Dane.

After a gruelling period of adjustment, they had discovered how to get along and were allowed to take the next step. Their sins had been atoned for, and although he tried to hide it from his minions, had brought a tear to his eye. So, he had asked the sky posse if they were interested in them.

Even though they had been given a second chance, others were bloody-minded and had no intention of changing. They spurned their chance and carried on regardless, so the basement horde were promptly messaged about their availability.

It had taken Claude some time yet now he had an indication of why both sides had taken a combative stance. In an attempt to wind each other up, gain supporters and cause general havoc, it appeared that a covert operative from both sides had been put on the Earth. Why each faction had to do this from time to time was beyond him. Were they just bored? Was it a test? Was it punishment because his latest Ofdead report was not satisfactory?

Flaming Ofdead.

The occasional faux pas by Death had resulted in a few poor sods being unintentionally shown a glimpse into the hereafter. Once Ofdead got wind of these lapses these unfortunates were scrambled back to their impending life with immediate effect. They always came soaring back from the brink, babbling about Heaven or Hell or God or Satan and spouting nonsense of how they had been specifically chosen to return. More often than not, these types went on to become conceited spiritual maniacs spreading the word of whatever being they had witnessed, as well as steering wayward teenagers into their beds.

Claude recognised the Grim Reaper (or as he knew her – Edna) should not have been doing her bloody reaping anywhere near these individuals but she was ever so apologetic for any misdemeanours. After millennia's, she was getting on and it was sadly showing yet she was still so happy in her work. There was no finer example that you get out of your demise what you put into it. It was such a shame as she was an absolute treasure, going about her daily business with a cheery smile on her face. The question of Edna's alias was a meeting to remember but 'The Light-hearted Reaper' didn't seem to sit right with some. Others thought it might be a nice way to greet your oncoming departure, but the majority opted for the more formidable title.

Whether it was boredom, a test or his Ofdead report, it was time to sort out this unholy and indeed holy mess, but another issue arose. Kevin.

He shouldn't be here!

Yet here he was, doing his worst. This was getting serious, and Claude knew his job was on the line.

The shit had clearly hit the fan and a disgruntled top brass from both sides had ordered the fan into action. The fan's name was Kevin and when Kevin got speaking you were done for. He spouted drivel to anyone unluckily within earshot about why Raith Rovers were the greatest football team to have existed. Before you knew what had happened, a breathtaking boredom had lured you into a trance, then slumber followed by the deepest comatose sleep known to the limboverse.

Kevin had become something of a celebrity in his own right, being referred to as 'The Sandman'. This moniker was not given by blowing magical grit into your eyes (which in all likelihood would do the exact opposite of sending you to sleep) and dispatching you off to some fanciful dreamworld. It was due to him making you feel like you were trudging through exhausting, energy-sucking sand striving to escape his ball sport related chit-chat. Kevin tended to be rolled out for unruly kids on Christmas Eve as a little gift for shattered parents.

Kevin was the ultimate incentive in keeping officialdom running tiptop. Claude realised that Kevin had been introduced to send Purgatory to sleep and judging by the proportion of snoozing personel on the shop floor, he seemed to be having a decent go. If successful, then it was time for a mass culling of the workforce.

Finally, Claude's luck changed. He had a positive hit.

He had found the two culprits - Donald Trump and Piers Morgan. They had gotten cocky and made mistakes. What gave them both away was that Trump was far too honest for his own good and Morgan was the devil incarnate. He was slightly aghast that he hadn't noticed them before, but he wasn't omnipresent and what was the point of him having staff?

Maybe, it was time to shake things up, give some a kick up the backside or put them on more rigorous training courses?

An innovative new method called 'How To Spot A Bad One on Earth' had just started by a lovely Yorkshire chap called Seth. His lectures were entertaining and always bought a titter from the students as he announced, 'Welcome t' 'ow t' spot a bad 'un on't that there Earth'. The advertisement poster showed a hand holding a pointer helpfully aiming at a picture of the Earth just in case anyone was unsure which planet they were dealing with. After this recent episode, Claude thought he might recommend a few employees.

He was going to have to bring this undercover terrestrial pairing down a peg or two as they were both getting gravely close to reaching the zenith of power. Unbeknown to most, Piers Morgan was within a cat's whisker of ruling the world. If he had presented early morning TV for another week then life as we know it would have been over.

Claude noticed that his staff began to stir as Kevin had quietened down to a low mumble. With a sigh of relief, he knew uniformity would reign once again. The crisis was over.

Claude's reward for the newly equitable truce was music - the purest of noise. Praise came from the choral choirs above and the diabolic chants from below. When the hailing from above met the incantations from below, they unified into the most exquisite sound imaginable. It was worth all his troubles. The combined melodies flowed over him, sent charged pulsations down his spine, and infused the euphony into his very bones. He was enchanted into a sublime, harmonious bubble experiencing the pinnacle of pleasure.

He had always triumphed in stopping hostilities once the problem had been detected. He was a damned but contented soul and he walked with a confident swagger, safe in the knowledge that he was good at this job. After all, he was the Middleman - the man that can.

Damian Tarnowski

Jonathan Vidgop

Translated into English by Mr. Leo Shtutin

In darkness

As you walk unlit nocturnal streets, your sense of time drains away by degrees. You cannot so much as say what o'clock it is. Is it late evening, or the dead of night? The city is dispeopled. Here and there windows glow dim, lone pedestrians scurry down back alleys.

Navigation by the stars is not a skill you possess, and you are lost—utterly lost amid the fathomless wastes of this dead city. These mute houses, these towers pockmarked with blind windows loom over you from every side, akin to stone tombs wherein pharaohs have been interred together with their hats and their umbrellas, their hand fans and their attachés.

You grow convinced morning will never arrive—such is the thickness of this murk. Its coming would, at any rate, be of little consequence to you: having survived the night, lost and defenceless, you could take no pleasure in the clamour of the day, and no pleasure, either, in its bright ringing sunlight, its bowler-hatted rushers-by, its hurtling motor cars, its big-head shout-mouth children, its crinolined wenches and deranged mothers and streetcorner policemen.

You wander ever onward through the dark, dispeopled city. When at last you can bear this torture no more, you approach the nearest house. A scrape, a knock at the solid oak door; someone swings it open, and you're momentarily blinded by the electric light pouring from the hall within. The hall is thronged with revellers, men and women making merry as if doing so were the most natural thing on earth. They whisper, chortle, gabble. They eat, they swish their skirts, they dance the paso doble, their revelry illuminated by bright lamps.

Why they've gathered here they themselves don't know. But still they rollick, still they titter, still they wink. What goes on in the night, beyond the walls of their bright-lit apartment, is no concern of theirs. How's that silence out there? No matter: inside, they're laughing like drains. Perhaps, in fact, they have gathered here purely so as not be in the dark.

You stand there, back pressed against an illumined wall. Sooner or later they must go their separate ways, must leave this safe haven behind. Unlikely that they'll keep up their unbridled merrymaking until morning. Out they'll hasten, hunched against the darkness, singly. Their smiles will slip from their painted faces, their laughter will wane, and their legs will hurry-scurry them into the murk. But before they manage to dart mouselike into their buildings, each of them will be devoured by the rapacious night.

Joseph Farley

The circus came to town

The last time the circus came to our small town, it was different from all the times it came before.

During previous visits, the circus folk set up big tents on a vacant lot and held a small parade to advertise their presence. Children would flock to the ticket booth dragging parents along. There would be popcorn dripping with butter or caramel, elephants and lions, trapeze artists, trick riders, magicians, tight rope walking, tumblers, and dozens of clowns.

The circus would stay in town a week or two, then pack up and leave, promising to return the following summer. Children would sigh and wave goodbye as the circus train pulled away from the station.

That was then. That was as it had always been for as long as anyone could remember. It was what was expected, what we knew, what we trusted in.

All that changed the last time the circus came to town, because it and its assemblage of performers, trainers, hostlers, pitchmen, canvas men and ticket sellers did not leave.

There was talk of diminished sales. Reduced bookings, increased costs for travel, wages, and animal feed. The circus, so people said, was kaput.

That all might have been true. No one in town was really certain. The circus people would clam up about it if you asked any of them. The fact was the circus did not leave.

Nor did it seem to disband. Not really. It was more as if it changed from a tightly run organization into a loose confederation, an association of fellow travelers. The circus did not leave. Nor did the circus people try much, for the most part, to blend in with the way things were in town, the way things had been since before grandad's grandad.

There were no attempts by the clowns to live without red round noses or pancake makeup. The trapeze artists walked around in their tights. The tumblers cartwheeled along the sidewalk instead of walking. Magicians insisted on pulling coins out of bus drivers' ears in order to pay their fares.

Tightrope walkers set up homes in apartments on opposite sides of Main Street, in ten story buildings, on the top floors. They strung wires between the buildings. They could be seen by the ant people down below on the street, walking high overhead. The tightrope walkers would set up chairs on their wires, and sit down, balancing while they read the morning newspaper. They would walk across the wires to visit each other's units. They hung their laundry out there to dry, carefully stepping over it as they went about their business. The smokers among them climbed out of apartment windows at all hours of day and night to puff on pipes, cigarettes and cigars while pacing along their beloved wires. When they flicked their ashes, the burning bits floated down damaging bonnets, hats, overcoats, and, in summer, bare heads and shoulders, of normal pedestrians.

Jugglers found work in grocery stores. While entertaining to watch, they tended to bruise the fruit and sometimes dropped the eggs. Actually, they rarely dropped anything, including the eggs. Still, there were enough witnesses to small disasters happening on occasion that the tales of splatterings could not be dismissed.

The ring master took a job as a schoolteacher. He became involved in politics on the side. He made no secret of his plans to run for mayor in the next election. All the clowns are working to rally voters to his side. The clowns seem to think they will all get government jobs if the ring master wins. If he does they will be able to stop entertaining at birthday parties and being counter help at local fast food restaurants.

Residents such as me, with roots, real roots in our town that go back generations, have been dismayed by all these changes. The character of our town is different. It is not what it was. Our youth have proven highly susceptible to the influence of these newcomers. It has become fashionable among teenagers to wear red noses, baggy pants, and oversized shoes. It has been one more disheartening development.

The wearing of tights, the frequency of neighbors attempting to produce flowers or an endless stream of multicolored handkerchiefs from a hat or sleeve nowadays strikes me as quite vulgar.

We are losing our sense of who we are or who we were.

Disgraceful really. We do not need all these tightropes springing up between a house and a garage. We are still capable of walking on the ground, thank you. As a doctor I have seen too many broken bones from sad attempts to emulate neighbors with better senses of balance.

I fear that we are slowly becoming members of the circus instead of the circus becoming part of our community.

I do not know what can be done about it. When I tried to speak up about my concerns at the most recent public meeting at the town hall, I was pelted with cream pies and nearly drowned in seltzer water.

It is not like I have issues with all the circus folk.

I said before, some made efforts to fit in. The lions, for example, have found respectable employment as security guards on the outside steps of the town library. They sit there all day watching who goes in and out. The elephants are doing well in the local logging industry. They have become welcome members of the town's Republican Club. As for much of the rest of these circus folk, I do not know what to say.

I have been told by more than one of the newcomers and their young admirers that I am narrow minded and old fashioned. I have been told I should leave town, leave my home, the place of my birth, the source of all my memories. I have even been threatened with being shot out of a cannon into a nearby suburb.

The police have stopped listening to my complaints. They are watching the opinion polls about the next election. There is a good chance that ring master will become their new boss. He has promised to give all the officers a raise.

Must I learn to juggle at my age? Become a clown? I am far too old to be an acrobat.

It is all coming to wrack and ruin. I fear for my future, the future of my hometown, the entire county, even the state.

Still, as bad as it has become, I have to admit the circus folk have brought some positive changes to our town. There are plenty of popcorn and cotton candy vendors now. That helps the economy I guess. Besides being plentiful, the popcorn now seems to taste better than what was available before. I especially like the caramel kind, even though it is bad for my bridge work.

You will have to come and see for yourself. I have to get off the phone. There are some clowns outside my door honking horns. I think they want me to sign a petition they want me to sign. They can be quite persistent. I had better see to them. I had better go and speak with them. I don't want to get pied again.

Joseph Farley

Aaron Becker

Section 23

The Balearic waves rolled along continuously, timelessly; oblivious to yesterday's disappointments and tomorrow's expectations. No respecter of reputations. Indifferent to time of year, spirit and mood. Heedless of the unemployed, ungratified, unmoving 23-year-old who lay before it, wondering what his next move might be. Having been discharged from his job at the *La Cubierta* bar for repeatedly swearing at a customer, Tyler spent the whole of Sunday evening imbibing alcohol, clad in a hybrid of sportswear and ruffian attire. His pockets contained minimal money; the sense he was now a depleted force was being slowly confirmed.

As the sun set on *Playa es Pouet* beach, he could see a group of tourists strolling and laughing together. He stood up.

"What the f**k are you looking at?"

They continued to laugh, more in bemusement than derision. Tyler responded by hurling an empty WKD bottle in their direction; they panicked and took flight. A few minutes later, his phone bleeped: '13-4-13-1' flashed across the screen. He knew what that meant.

Inside room 23 of the *Adelino Hotel* on the *Carrer de la Mar*, a palpable air of bonhomie that went beyond conventional description could be found. Tyler and his old football teammate Makenzie were painting Monday's predawn hours a vivid shade of hedonism; with their plenteous cigarettes and alcohol came the addendum of blue ecstasy pills. '13-4-13-1' was their code for obtaining the latter – the numbers derived from the initials of MDMA, its substrate.

"What am I gonna do now, fam?"

"Just wait until you've heard my idea..."

By reference to their own well-established paradigms of opinion, the boys derogated everyone who had damaged their lives in however minor a way – "this t**t at the children's home", "that c**t who got me busted one time" – and went about formulating their grand plan. Tyler accepted that his 'criminal mastermind' persona existed primarily in his own imagination, and agreed with Makenzie that his last drops of hope were going to be used up on this mission; fear and anxiety would have to be checked at the door!

24 hours later, another E ensured Tyler retained that anything-is-possible glow which accompanies the peak of its use – a sensation from a different, higher orbit. The metronomic rhythms of the night-time ocean continued below the *Mirador de sa Punta*, as he attempted to execute Makenzie's plan.

As those who shared his company during afterparties quickly discovered, the 'high' version of Tyler brimmed with self-assurance. On this occasion however, his confidence became cocksureness. He had never intended to kill the passer-by, instinctively using his gun once his victim had produced a weapon of his own. The copious cash Tyler purloined was scant solace; things had now taken a turn for the surreal.

It was Tyler's turn to panic when a road sweeper trundled down the lane towards him. He sprinted away, carrying his firearm, only for his much-sweatier-than-usual hands to unintentionally drop it into a nearby drain. As he hid in the gardens of the *Bellamar Hotel*, he knew this error was patent, pungent and prescient. Time, not unlike those Ibizan tides, could never grant the request of those who wished to turn it back.

On warm weekends such as this, Ibiza specialised in bursts of colour – the heavenly blue of the ocean, the adjoining crisp golden sand, the pure white exterior of edifices upon clifftops, set against the cerulean sky. Tyler voraciously finished off his breakfast in the *Adelino* dining room: eggs, bacon, mushrooms, sausages, grilled tomatoes, fried bread, hash browns. A porcelain cup of dark roast coffee provided the perfect adjunct on the side, but the victuals were not uppermost in his and Makenzie's thoughts.

"That gun's got my prints all over it. Who can help me get off the island before it gets traced back to me? It's only a matter of time…"

"Look, I can only think of one name, blud."

"Yeah?"

"Shay Kullom. I used to know him, he might still know me…it's a long shot but he's defo got the connections."

"Calm! Got a number?"

"Nah, not any more. There's a place you could try, though?"

"Oh…"

"The bar where they all watch the sunset."

"*Café del Mar*?"

A festival of flowers – astilbe, buddleia, cosmos, delphiniums and echinops among them – imparted greater colour to proceedings, as Tyler strutted down the sun-saturated *Carrer de Londres*, more on his mind than in it. As far as the ostensibly higher echelons of gangland were concerned, he may well be pressing some ill-advised buttons by even mentioning Mr Kullom's name. Yet if he still envisaged himself gatecrashing the mainland with his rebelliousness intact, what other option was there?

"What can I get you?"

The Balearic purism that once defined *Café del Mar* had been superseded by a rather more commercial set of values, yet the old character remained nonetheless.

"I'm looking for Shay Kullom."

"One moment, please."

When a suitably furtive-looking individual appeared a few moments later, Tyler knew those powers of persuasion would be called upon, and some, at this point of reckoning.

"I need to get off the island asap, I'm willing to do any…"

"Alright look, he runs *Club Nàutic* these days – that's your best bet. Tell him the Operator General sent you."

Tyler thanked his mystery assister and asked for a cocktail on the house, receiving in reply a hollow laugh.

Tyler beamed and looked down at his boxer shorts, the only garment he was wearing, as the saturnalia around him continued. Every corner of the hilltop cottage overlooking *Cala Gració* rented by Bailey – the goalkeeper in his and Makenzie's football team – was buzzing and alive with activity, soundtracked by a compilation of Ibiza trance classics. Makenzie was deep in conversation on the far side of the room with Clayton, who'd had a tick shaven into the side of his hair as a forfeit for losing their version of 'Play Your Cards Right'; others opted to down an entire bottle of spirits, engrave a rude word upon their hands in permanent marker or simply strip off, as Tyler had done. Bailey himself was slumped on the floor, barely intelligible, amongst a sea of cans, balloons, straws, pills and trainers.

The quest to find Shay Kullom was reaching a crescendo, not unlike the mid-point of those trance anthems; local radio reports made it clear that the murder investigation wasn't going to be faded out – as trance records often are – and having already proved himself to be an assured player of the networking game, Tyler was ready for his challenge. As he left the farewell rave, Jackson offered him a pearl of wisdom:

"Do not touch the pack…you might not ever come back!"

Club Nàutic was the kind of place that orthodox categories could not begin to describe; a bar, nightclub, casino, sports hall and bordello all in one. Upon being searched and asked why he had visited, Tyler – not exactly accustomed to such opulent environs – reeled off a neatly phrased variant of his on-the-run narrative, illustrated with a credible backstory.

"I don't care if the Operator General sent you here", snarled the security man. "Shay Kullom doesn't do charities. Run along now!"

Tyler pleaded and protested, his voice distorted to the point of unrecognisability by anxiety. He found himself ejected, catching the eye of a heavily inebriated teenager on the way out. Tyler engaged him in conversation, expounding his predicament.

"Shay might be able to help you there, G – if he likes ya."

"Do you know of anyone else who's connected to him?"

"Well, yeh. I know a girl called Elsa, she's his partner. As far as I know, she lives at *Villa Can Jasa*. Section 23, I think."

Tyler recorded the stripling's slurred words on his phone, so as not to forget them later. As he thanked the teenager, Tyler was handed a blue gemstone for luck.

Next stop: *Villa Can Jasa*. Circumstances of real uncertainty had become circumstances of real anticipation; could Tyler have gained enough momentum to extend his escape into at least another 24 hours?

"Shay Kullom's with me", said the young lady who greeted Tyler at the section to which he'd been directed.

"You must be Elsa, then?"

Relief pervaded through Tyler's body when she answered in the affirmative. However, after bestowing more information upon her, Tyler was downcast at hearing that Shay had not been seen for several days, and in any event was living under an alias. An unwritten rule of criminality is that one is always permitted to forge a new outward identity, as Tyler himself had done at various junctures.

"Look, if you really want to track him down, I might be able to give you an address…but how do I know you went to *Club Nàutic*? You look like someone who'd get barred from there!"

Tyler's proclivity for bursts of contumely thankfully took a leave of absence, as he calmly produced the gemstone, which could not have been found anywhere else on the island. It was soon joined in his tracksuit pocket by a post-it note.

Several light years away from the potent kind of intimacy offered by Bailey's cottage was the putative address of Shay Kullom. Tyler's heart rate accelerated as his taxi driver took him towards the mountainous village of *Sant Josep de sa Talaia*: the final foray into the deeper reaches of the island's underworld.

At times his obstreperous, no-holds-barred heart-on-sleeve personality made him seem vulgar or one-dimensional – as he continued to use obsolete words and appoint himself witness to the unspecified "good old days" – but at certain other times his fearless passion served him well and brought others around to his side. This had to be one of those times.

At Tyler's request, the driver played an old *Café del Mar* compilation CD, providing a soundtrack to this final attempt to break the logjam, this date with destiny. When he got out of the taxi, Tyler – dosed to the gills with adrenaline, refusing to believe his best chance of absquatulation had come and gone – felt powered forward by a renewed intensity, mobilised for battle once more.

A heavily armed cadre of security guards met Tyler at the gate of what appeared to be a villa, the *Solar House*. He felt the comfort of the gemstone in his pocket once more.

"I'm here to see Shay Kullom." There followed the now-familiar backstory, modified slightly for its new audience.

"I believe what you're saying," answered one of the guards. Progress at last!

"But I'm afraid that won't be possible", the voice continued coldly.

Tyler's eyebrows raised. He was about to devise a response when the guard interposed.

"Unfortunately, he is dead. Nobody can live forever, you know".

A look of shock imbued Tyler's face. "What? How?"

"You see, someone killed him...shot him dead...last Monday night...near the *Mirador de sa Punta*...haven't you heard?"

Aaron Becker

Zary Fekete

Rhythm of the Train

The man wondered, what would the city be like? He'd never been there, but he'd had time enough to think about it. As the train carried him through the countryside, he spent hour after hour visualizing it. He pictured the moment he would see the city rising up on the horizon. He imagined the skyscrapers almost touching the clouds. He thought about the city's wide streets and leafy parks.

The first day on board the train he walked up and down the narrow corridor which connected the compartments. He met many other travelers. The kindly older couple in the cabin next to his planned to get off at the next station; a small village. It was where their daughter lived, they told him. She would meet them at the station and then bring them to her cabin up in the woods. When he told them about his city, they marveled and said they hoped he'd find the place everything he'd dreamed it might be.

He met all the young people in the cabin three doors down from him. They were going on, past his city, to some destination along the coast. There was a beach event happening there and the young folks chattered about it with excitement. There would be dancing and lots of food. Their sunny smiles seemed filled with glittering sand and sunshine. They had plenty of energy and they slapped each other on the backs and laughed at each other's jokes. He mentioned his city to them and they smiled politely. They told him they'd heard of people who had gotten off at his city and had a fine time there.

He looked out the train window at the countryside flashing by. The train passed several small villages. He saw people driving cows to pasture and big wagons bringing in hay. From time to time the train crossed a river and he saw fisherman on the water and great barges floating by.

He thought about his first day in the city. He meant to get off the train and put his luggage in a locker. With no baggage he'd be free to explore. He wanted to eat a good meal. He meant to take in several parks and smell the flowers. Toward evening he thought he might stroll along the river walk. Perhaps he'd meet someone. They might have dinner together.

When evening came he walked down to the dining car with the rest of the people. Music was piped in through the speaker system. The lively melodies gave the food a festive quality. Some of the young people got up to dance. Nothing raunchy. Just young people having fun. And then, after the rhythm of the train settled into its nightly lull, everyone drifted back to their own compartments. He lay down on his bunk after he changed into his pajamas and felt the gentle back and forth of the tracks below the train. He fell asleep thinking of his city.

He woke sometime later. Something in the car's rhythm had changed. He felt the movement of the train, but there was no tick tick of the rails beneath him. He hopped up opened his cabin door, still in his pajamas. When he looked out the train window his mouth fell open. The countryside was gone. There were no villages flashing by, no people. It was nothing but vast, yellow dunes of sand. The train seemed to be sailing on it like a boat.

He knocked at the older couple's door but got no answer. He moved down to the young folks' compartment. They were all just waking.

What happened, he asked them?

They didn't seem alarmed. Trains change, they said.

What will you do, he asked?

It will be fine, they said. There's bound to be a party or two waiting up ahead. And even if there isn't, this place is just as good as any other.

He left the young people with a sense of desperation growing within him. He saw the conductor coming down.

He rushed up to him and asked about the older couple.

They got off about an hour ago, the conductor said.

But where did they go?

The conductor shrugged.

How much farther to the city?

No city now, the conductor said. Nothing but this, he gestured out the window at the vast desert moving by.

The conductor continued down the corridor. The man looked out the window at the dunes. He felt he could feel the heat baking on them. The brightness of the sun hurt his eyes. He squinted painfully, searching the sand as it whizzed past. There was nothing but miles of waste.

He walked back to his cabin. As he walked he felt pain in his joints. The piercing sun outside his window was blinding. He pulled the shade. He lay down on his bunk, wincing from an ache in his back. His body felt strange to him. He lay on his bunk, feeling the rhythm of the train. Slowly he fell asleep.

Zary Fekete

Tim Frank

Losing the Will to Live by Tim Frank

The Wigwam motel on the edge of town is filled with the Fridborg family from all across the country, ready for uncle Terry's birthday bash.

Bored, some eavesdrop on each other through paper thin walls, ignoring the bedbugs teeming around their feet. Others flip coins into a cup, while some pick at their bleeding gums.

In the motel carpark a couple of Terry's cousins quench their thirst with Bud Light. They sit on crates by a fire, playing violins. They burn Wigwam postcards and tourist maps, all stolen from the souvenir shop.

Grandma sits on the porch wearing a cowboy hat and boots. The weather is well below zero but she doesn't care, she just knits a bobble hat and spits at spiders' webs.

At night Terry's nephews wrestle by the motel swimming pool, then take turns to peer through binoculars at the centre of town. It sparkles like a cluster of satellites under a quarter moon. The nephews are frustrated, they want to stroll through the city and see the sights, see life. They're sick of their weird family.

The day of the party arrives and the motel function room is arranged with tables and chairs. There's a giant pork joint with crackling, goose fat potatoes, buckets of sloppy cranberry sauce, and a three tier birthday cake for dessert.

Before dinner, everyone is asked to stand and share their story, as if they were in an AA meeting. Francine, Uncle Terry's second cousin, climbs onto the table and recites her sexual history like an emcee at a boxing match. She shuffles around, knocking over crystal glasses, kicking the gravy boat and then in a moment of panic, she makes the most important announcement of her life.

"I'm in love with Uncle Terry!" she says.

Unfortunately, he has no feelings for her – she looks like cousin Otto and her feet are swollen like blowfish. Uncle Terry rushes outside to smoke a cigarette under an aggressive sky, holding his breath for as long as he can, losing the will to live.

Francine scuttles into the carpark and spots him warming himself in his Ford Mondeo, draining his car battery. When he sees her wave at him, he revs the engine and disappears down the hill, swallowed up by the city. He doesn't look back.

Francine's heart bursts and she collapses to her knees in despair. A little dramatic maybe, but that's how she feels.

But soon enough the party will be over and the family will disperse back to their homes. They will lock themselves away and try to forget the motel, with the ghostly shadows lurking inside their rooms, the smell of kerosene emerging from their bathrooms, and the screaming from the highway opposite.

Francine copes with it all by burning her gas bills, her driving license, and everything that proves she's a Fridborg, then she balls up her feelings and buries them deep inside her stomach. In time she will forget Uncle Terry with his charcoal eyes and sallow cheekbones — and when her ordeal is over, she will fall in love with the very first man she meets.

Jim Bates

Frozen Fingers

The wind howled down the canyon. Above the granite walls, the leaden sky leaked snowflakes that swirled around the two figures huddled on their knees against the cold. They needed to get a fire going. Fast. Before it was too late.

"Jerry, how are those matches holding up?" Steve asked. He had his gloves off and was blowing on his frozen hands. His fingers were turning white and he was losing all feeling in them. "Can you get that kindling lit?"

Shit, no," Jerry swore, his frosted breath immediately turning to ice, adding to the frozen mass building on his beard and mustache. "I've got three left and I can't feel my fingers to hold them. Can't feel a damn thing." He blew on his hand to emphasize his point.

Those were not the words Steve wanted to hear. It was twenty degrees below zero. If they didn't get a fire going in the next few minutes hypothermia would set in and they'd begin the slow agonizing process of freezing to death. He blinked to keep his watering eyes from freezing shut. It didn't help. He had to rub at them to finally clear his vision.

Next to the two men the rushing water of the Yellow Knife River cascaded over ice-covered boulders on its way to Lake Superior ten miles to the east. Steve and Jerry had been on a winter hiking trip along the trail that ran high above the river when the ledge of snow they were on collapsed, and they tumbled thirty feet down the steep slope into the frigid water below. In just seconds their heavy winter clothing, Jerry's dark blue thermal pants and parka, and Steve's tan Carhartt overalls and insulated jacket, were soaked through to their skin. The wet clothing and the numbing cold together were a dangerous combination.

They had scrambled out and found a level spot in the snow where they took stock of their predicament. Their day packs were lost and Steve had sprained his wrist. Jerry had wrapped it as well as he could with a wet scarf, but it didn't help much. One consolation was that the cold helped numb the pain, but that was all. Steve could feel his beard icing up and, with his face getting numb, it was getting hard to speak. He wasn't much help. It was up to Jerry to build the fire.

They'd constructed a small teepee of twigs and pine needles but a combination of wet stick matches and a wind swirling down the narrow canyon walls made getting the match lit next to impossible. With two matches to go, their prospects were grim.

Steve shuffled on his knees closer to Jerry, their heavy clothes forming a barrier from the wind. Then, in a gesture of profound intimacy, he motioned to his friend, "Here, give me your hands."

When Jerry balked, Steve said, "Don't give me that macho BS." He motioned again and said, softly, "Here, let me help." Steve took his friend's bare hands in his and, ignoring the pain in his wrist, drew them to his lips and blew on them, warming them with his breath.

The warm air melted the ice on Jerry's hands and it dripped onto the snow, freezing immediately. Blood flowed into his fingers bringing them back to life. After a few more seconds, he could wiggle them. "Hey, man, good going. They're better." He flexed his hand. "I can feel my fingers, now."

Steve blew one last long breath on his friend's fingers before Jerry quickly moved his hands away. He grabbed a match and in one swift motion struck it against the side of the matchbox. Nothing happened. It was too wet. On the second try, it broke apart and fell to the snow, useless.

The two men looked at each other, each doing all they could to tamp down their mounting terror. Unless they got a fire going, and soon, they were going to die.

"Here, Jer," Steve said, softly. "Give me your hands again."

"Okay." Though from the cold, Jerry extended his arms.

Steve again cupped his friend's fingers and blew on them, willing warmth from the core of his body into them. Their faces were windblown and red. Their teeth were chattering and their eyes watering so much they kept freezing shut. Their beards were filled with chunks of ice. And they only had one match left.

The sun was setting behind the pine trees lining the rim of the canyon. With the lack of sunlight, the cold was settling in deep and hard.

Steve blew on Jerry's fingers one last time. "Ready?"

"Yeah." Jerry quickly reached for the last match. He held it as tight as he could, resolve set in his eyes. He looked at Steve. "Let's do this."

"Go for it, man."

Jerry struck the match. Both men watched, their lives hanging in the balance. A gust of wind blew past them. *Oh, no.* The flame flickered...then faded....then caught.

In spite of their ice-covered beards and frozen faces, the two men looked at each other and grinned.

Then they quickly set about building a roaring fire.

Jim Bates

Paul McAllister

The Magician's Assistant

I didn't have time to study the building and compare my memories of it with how it was today. A young man emerged from the entrance doors, descended the steps and politely but firmly demanded to know my business.

At first, I didn't realise this was the janitor. When I did realise, I wondered: *How did that happen? How did school janitors become younger than me?*

He escorted me to a room at the school's far end, following a route that avoided the classroom windows and ensured I saw no children and no children saw me. I remembered the room as being the headmistress's office, her sanctuary when she wasn't teaching. Now it was occupied by a secretary who, like the janitor, was many years my junior. She was keen to find out my business too.

One wall of the office supported a gallery of framed photographs of past headmistresses, including Mrs Dunlop. Pictured in monochrome, with granny glasses and a bun of grey hair, she looked like she'd run the school in the wrong seventies – the 1870s, not the 1970s.

While the secretary questioned me and, I knew, the janitor hovered just outside the door, I thought it ironic that during her reign as headmistress Mrs Dunlop had probably never devoted a thought to child safety. The idea that certain people might intend kids harm had likely never occurred to her. That at a time when the Troubles were at their worst, when between them Catholic terrorists, Protestant terrorists, British soldiers and local security-forces members were killing two to three hundred people a year.

She let *anyone* into the school. For example, the man and woman who rolled into the playground one morning in a big van with not just back-doors but doors on the sides too. When they'd parked and the teachers had herded us around, the couple lifted up the side-doors and propped them on poles so we could see their van's interior. It contained shelves lined with meshed-wire cages. In these were animals we knew, like rabbits, guinea pigs and tortoises, and other animals we didn't – little monkey-creatures with black patches on their eyes and white-and-black ringed tails, or tiny things, also monkey-like, with fluffy heads and creepily human faces. The man and woman took those exotic animals from their cages and tried to make them perform for us, which mainly involved poking them with sticks till they reacted by wailing and screeching.

The van exuded a reek of fur, straw and dung. While they tormented one of the monkey-things, the stench and the animal's screeching became too much for me and I started crying. One of the teachers – not Mrs Dunlop, who was responsible for the older classes, but Mrs Daley, who looked after the P1s, 2s and 3s – hurried over. Wretchedly, I raised a hand. But she seized my *other* hand and dragged me into the school.

Another example – the puppeteer. He commandeered a classroom, filled one half of it with rows of chairs and made it an auditorium, and used a teacher's table as a stage. He placed a cassette player on one end of his table-stage and a black case on the other, then climbed up onto it. For his show, he played a medley of tunes and took from the case a succession of marionettes, whom he made dance to each tune, on the tabletop, before his feet.

The marionettes included a skeleton that did a goofy dance to some xylophone music. The youngest pupils, like me, were sitting in the front row of chairs. At the climax of the xylophone dance, the puppeteer suddenly swung the skeleton off the table and into our faces. Into *my* face.

My reaction? Again, I exploded into tears.

And again Mrs Daley sped towards me. She reached out and I lifted a hand to grasp hers, but she looked at me harshly. Despite my agitation, I realised my *faux pas* and lifted the other hand. She grabbed it and whisked me from the room.

Having found those visitors intimidating, I should have been terrified when we were informed we'd be getting a show the next afternoon from a magician. Yet I wasn't terrified, maybe because I felt a kinship with magicians – at least, with wizards and witches, because I'd been nicknamed after them.

I had Mrs Daley to thank for that. One morning we were copying sums into our jotters and, in a momentary lapse, I let my left hand use the pencil, not my right. Mrs Daley barked, "Proper hand, please!" She shook her head. "Ye're a lucky man ye weren't born hundreds a' years ago. Ye know what they thought about left-handed people then? They thought ye all practised witchcraft. Aye, they'd a' burnt ye at the stake!" My classmates found this hilarious. Afterwards, I was called 'Wizzy', short for 'wizard', and taunted about owning a wand, casting spells, and wearing a cloak and pointy hat covered in crescents and stars.

And the magician didn't seem threatening when we were seated for the show and Mrs Dunlop introduced him. He was almost cartoonishly round-faced, and had a long moustache that drooped sadly past the corners of his mouth, and his hair all clung to the sides of his head while a bare, pink disc of skin sat on its top. He looked even shorter than Mrs Dunlop and the grey topcoat he wore, which on an averagely-tall man would have stopped above the knees, went well below his.

He greeted us, then lifted a waste-paper bin, walked up to one of the boys and tweaked his nose. Immediately we heard a clatter of coins spraying down from his nose into the bin. He approached two more boys and did the same to them.

During the next half-hour he got Mrs Dunlop to provide and sign a pound note – pound notes were serious money in those days and only teachers carried them – before spiriting the note off into thin air, and then cut open an orange and extracted the same signed note from it. He showed us five big interlocking hoops that one moment were suddenly free of one another and bouncing randomly on the tabletop in front of him and the next moment were locked together in a chain again. He produced a silver globe that floated of its own accord, peeping over the top and around the sides of a sheet of cloth he held stretched out. He set on the table three trays of different-coloured sand, one orange, one green, one red, and mixed them in a bowl of water until they were a dark muddy mess, but then scooped out handfuls of the mixture and revealed that – hey presto! – one handful contained only orange sand, the next handful only green, the next only red.

And at one point he removed his topcoat, revealing a waistcoat covered in diamond-shaped patches of blue, pink and gold. He brought out a pack of playing cards and miraculously, with the cards and coat, he…

"Excuse me?"

While Mrs Dunlop's photograph transported me 50 years back to the couple with the mobile zoo, the puppeteer, the magician, I'd forgotten about the school secretary. "Excuse me?" she said again. I detected a note of hostility in her voice now. I'd become good at detecting that in people's voices.

"Yes?" I focused on her and tried to infuse my own voice with gentleness and reasonableness.

"I'm sorry, but we can't help ye. We're not authorised to agree to an event like that. Ye'd need to ask higher up, go to someone at the Education Authority in Omagh."

"I understand," I said. "Well, thank you so much for settin' me straight. I'll contact the Education Authority an' maybe one day soon we'll see each other again." I saw her wince ever-so-slightly at the idea, but maintained my smile and backed humbly out of her office.

The young janitor, who'd been so suspicious of me he'd skulked outside the office the whole time, escorted me back to the entrance. I gave him a polite 'thank you' and went down the steps to the playground.

I was in Mrs Daley's P3 class when the magician gave his first show. For a week afterwards, my schoolmates talked about nothing else. Well, except for the school's dozen Free Presbyterian pupils, whose parents had told Mrs Dunlop they had to sit out the show and spend the time in a different classroom. Their reasoning was that anyone promoting magic was a servant of the devil.

I noticed around then that people stopped calling me 'Wizzy'. Presumably this was because wizards, practitioners of magic, were now considered cool and I wasn't allowed a cool nickname. Instead, unimaginatively, they started calling me 'Lefty'.

The magician returned three years later. By then I was in P6 and my teacher was Mrs Dunlop. My left-handedness still caused problems. My parents had even sanctioned extra-curricular handwriting lessons where I stayed after the end of the school day and a disgruntled Mrs Dunlop supervised me while I copied out passages in joined-up handwriting, an oversized fountain pen clutched in my right hand.

During that P6 magic show I did something daring. When the magician took off his grey topcoat, revealing again the multi-coloured waistcoat of blue, pink and gold diamonds, and asked for a volunteer, I stuck up my arm – my right one, obviously. I managed to stick mine up first and a few moments later he was positioning me at the front where everyone could see me. He also made me put on his topcoat, which came even further down my legs than it did on his. Its cuffs covered my hands to their knuckles. I heard chuckles from the other schoolchildren, even the little ones, and realised how foolish I looked.

The magician produced a set of cards, fanned them and walked around showing them to various pupils. "Look closely," he said. "You see a normal deck of 52 playing cards." He gathered them into a single block and turned to me. "I'll leave these with our young friend here." He dropped the cards into an internal pocket behind the coat's right breast. My heart thumped heavily on the left side of my chest and I was glad he hadn't deposited the cards there, where he'd have felt my careering heartbeat.

Then he took out a second deck of cards and let the audience inspect them too. This time, however, he shuffled them and asked a P7 girl: "Young lady, could you take the top card and show it to us?" The girl raised the card in the air. From where I stood, I saw a rash of red spots.

"You all see? It's the Nine of Hearts." Then the magician asked me, "Could you, sir, reach into that coat-pocket and pick one card out of the deck I placed there? Then hold it up?"

I moved a hand towards the pocket – and froze. I'd fleetingly made eye-contact with Mrs Dunlop, who was sitting behind my schoolmates, and realised I was using my left hand. My *wrong* hand. So instead I groped up to the pocket, on the coat's right side, with my right hand. I fumbled, but found the pocket near the shoulder and dug out one of the cards.

I held it towards the audience but saw something was amiss. The nearest faces looked puzzled. When I glanced at the girl with the Nine of Hearts, she seemed particularly puzzled.

Briefly, the magician's plump face, behind his moustache, grimaced with displeasure. But only briefly. He declared, "And as you can see, it's the Two of Clubs. Which is what you'd expect. Because the magic in my coat hasn't started working yet. Now, let me activate the magic." He swirled a hand in the air above me, intoning, "Ala-kasham!" Then: "That should do it. Let's see what happens next!"

He got another pupil to fish a card out of his deck and hold it aloft – the Queen of Clubs – and instructed me to take another card from the pocket. This time he watched me closely and when I rummaged up with my right hand, he instructed, "Maybe use the other hand. It'll be easier." I withdrew my right hand, extended the left, and…

Again, I saw Mrs Dunlop, above the heads of my classmates.

At the last moment, I reverted to my right hand, fumbled in the pocket, found something and held it out. A disappointed sigh ran through the audience.

The grimace lasted longer on the magician's face this time. He removed the card from my trembling hand and said, "The Four of Spades… Son, how old are you?"

"Ten," I stammered.

"Hmm," he said. "I'd thought you were older. Maybe that's affecting the magic." He added in a whisper, "Use your left hand. Your right one must be unlucky."

He tried once more. Another schoolmate picked a card from his deck and I probed into the coat. My teeth were gritted with concentration, I ignored Mrs Dunlop, I made myself use my *left* hand. However, my hand found *two* flaps with *two* packs of cards in them. One was higher up and I probably wouldn't have encountered it if my hand hadn't been shaking so much. Which pocket and pack should I go for? I needed to decide fast. I picked the upper set of cards and removed one of them.

When I held it out, both the magician and audience sighed. He no longer looked annoyed, just resigned. "I'm sorry," he said, helping me out of the coat. "I don't know why, but the magic doesn't seem to *work* for you."

I'd crossed the playground and nearly reached the avenue that led down to the road when behind me a bell rang. Its shrill, electronic sound surprised me. Somehow, I'd thought that a teacher would still wave an old-fashioned hand-held bell. My pace slowed. Then I heard children begin to spill out through the entrance doors and down into the playground. I also heard an adult voice: "Be careful goin' down them steps!" These days, of course, someone had to be in the playground with them during breaktimes, making sure they were safe. In my time, Mrs Dunlop, Mrs Armstrong and Mrs Daley sat in the office and drank coffee, not giving a damn if outside we ran riot.

On my right was a strip of grass and then a fence, and up from the strip rose a line of poplar trees, planted sometime after my schooldays had ended. When I reached the last tree in the line, I stepped sideways, off the avenue and in behind it, so that I was no longer visible from the school.

A minute after I'd sat down, I felt a wetness on my face. And not just my face – the tears had already wormed their way past my chin, onto my throat, down to my shirt-collar. Mrs Dunlop noticed my tears at the same moment, hurried across, grasped my shoulder – no hands now – and shepherded me from the room. We left the magician doing his trick with the hoops that were sometimes locked together and sometimes weren't.

She left me outside the door of her office and reappeared with a box of paper hankies. They were called 'hankies' in those days, not 'tissues'. While she rubbed one over my face, she chided, "What's gotten into ye? Sobbin' yer eyes out just because his silly magic trick went wrong!"

She must have spoken loudly for then the door of the nearest classroom opened and Mrs Armstrong, the P4 and 5 teacher, came out to see what was wrong. She'd been given the task of minding the Free Presbyterian kids while they sat out the show. Behind her, a couple of small faces peeped around the doorpost. At the sight of my own stricken face, their expressions became smug.

Hadn't they tried to warn me? The magician was a servant of the devil.

A child's voice disturbed my recollections. "What are ye doin', Mister?" I looked out from behind the poplar tree and discovered four kids, P3 or P4 age, standing nearby on the grass.

I slid my coat off my shoulders and arms. "What am I doin'? Well, I'm goin' to show yous a trick."

The boy who'd spoken was made of stronger stuff than I'd been 50 years ago. He displayed no fear and soon stood next to the poplar tree with my topcoat draped around him. Its hem almost touched the grass and its cuffs almost swallowed his hands. I pushed up the left sleeve until his fingers were visible. "Ye'll need this free, to pick out the cards."

Meanwhile, from the direction of the school building, I heard shouts. I'd been spotted.

I planted one deck of cards inside the coat and waved a second pack at the three other children. "Quick!" I urged. "Pick a card. Any card!"

One child obliged. "Yous see it? The Four a' Diamonds." I turned back to the kid in the coat. "Now. Take a card from *your* pocket – "

Smoothly, his left hand dipped into the coat's inside pocket, on the right, removed a card and held it up. The kid who'd taken the Four of Diamonds from the second pack gave an appreciative gasp. So did the other kids. The boy in the coat turned his hand so he could see the card himself.

"Jaisus! It's the Four a' Diamonds too!"

The playground monitor had almost reached us. Her shouts had summoned the young janitor and he was running so hard he'd almost caught up with her. No time for any further tricks dependent on the dexterity, or lack of it, of the left and right hands. No time to even retrieve my coat. Happily, I swung around and sprinted towards the gates at the avenue's bottom.

After a lifetime of disappointments, I'd proven the magician wrong. The magic *did* work for me.

David Rudd

Ars Musica

Everyone knows the line about Proust dipping that confectioner's cake in his hot tea and being transported back to childhood. Some might find my vehicle of less refined, but the intensity of memory is no less.

My madeleine moment occurred recently, when I returned to my old secondary school, some thirty years after I'd been a pupil there. I was being lauded as a "famous old boy". However, the Proustian moment had nothing to do with the school itself. It occurred as I was waiting to leave, to be ferried to the local radio station. As I sat in the otherwise empty hall, a cleaner approached down the corridor and she — there's no other word for it — "burbled" as she came! I knew then, before she'd even entered, that it was Betty, whom I'd not seen in some twenty-five years.

We'd been neighbours on a council estate only a mile or so away. She and her husband, Tony, had moved into the house adjoining ours. In fact, for all I know, they might still be there. I'd have been about twelve, and Betty must have been in her mid-twenties. To my pubescent eyes, she was a goddess, and I could never understand why she'd married "Bellyache" — as I called him — a hulking, sallow-skinned man who had the grossest beer gut ever. Aside from his belly, and true to his nickname, Tony was always complaining. I used to pity Betty, thinking of that flabby walrus clambering on her.

To appreciate my madeleine moment, you need to know that there was a communal passageway between our houses, giving access to the backyards and gardens. Well, all those years ago, I'd been standing in our yard when I heard this crackling sound echoing through that arched passage. I presumed it was Bellyache, his putrid guts complaining about the fry-ups and kegs of ale he threw at them. I hid behind our dustbins. However, it was not Bellyache but Betty. Those resounding phwarps instantly turned mellifluous as, with a cigarette dangling from her lips, she emerged, dressed in a tight red skirt and white blouse.

So, some thirty odd years later, sitting there in my old school, it was those same dulcet tones that made their way along the corridor. I sat, mesmerised, as Betty entered and, spotting me there, strove to curb her windiness. Yet she gave no hint of recognition and, as for me, I was happy to remain anonymous. She spoke, but only to apologise for disturbing me.

She'd certainly changed. Gone was that svelte young figure I lusted after. Childbearing and a crap diet, I supposed. Little did she know what I owed her — and, if she did, she'd have been even more embarrassed!

How many times had Betty sparked my fantasies? Countless were the daydreams where I'd rescued her from Bellyache, thence to have her throw her arms around me and lead me into her parlour. Even today, those imaginary scenarios stirred something. Back then, I was permanently aroused. I'd be up in my room, practising my music (I was a bit of a prodigy) when thoughts of Betty would take over. After a while, hearing no flute playing, Mum would call up to see I was alright. "Just polishing my pipe," I'd respond (my standard euphemism!), peaking round the curtains at Betty, outside.

Seeing her hang out the washing was a favourite pastime. She'd bend to her clothes basket, her buttocks ripe as a peach. Then she'd stand and peg something out. Her skirt would rise, revealing nylon-encased flesh and, sometimes, more: stocking tops, suspenders, bare skin!

So taken was I with her figure that it was a while before I even noticed the clothes themselves. For there, lost amongst Bellyache's capacious Y-fronts and huge string vests, danced Betty's underthings: black knickers with matching bras, underskirts and suspender belts. The very idea of that material hugging her contours brought me to boiling point.

After she'd finished pegging her clothes, Betty would take a turn round their garden, weed-infested though it was. When her hazel eyes caught sight of a dandelion clock (and their garden was full of them), her smile was radiant. Gently, she'd pick it and, pursing those full lips of hers, disseminate those seedheads. Like the smoke from her cigarettes, she'd watch them swirl away.

Despite the ecstasy of spying on Betty from my room, it lacked one crucial dimension: the ars musica of Betty herself; that magnificent fanfare with which she announced her presence. Fortunately, I had other places from which to eavesdrop, my favourite being halfway down our garden, in Dad's vegetable patch. The taller veg — corn, peas, string beans — provided good hiding places, and a solid horticultural alibi, too. This said, I don't think Betty ever spotted me.

Sunday afternoons were best, when Bellyache was down at The Red Lion for his lunchtime session. Strains of a brass ensemble would drift across from our local bandstand, but they couldn't hold a candle to Betty. She'd amble down the garden, her melodious tones merging with the garden's soundscape of insect and birdsong: mellow trills and cheeky chirrups, flutes tootling, tubas wheezing, horns parping. It was all I could do not to applaud, inspired — no doubt— by the self-congratulatory claps with which Betty punctuated her own performance.

It's hard now to describe, but that wasteland of hers became a paradise. Each sweet peep and chirp seeming to emanate from the flora and fauna itself, stirred, no doubt, to sing her praises.

As was I! And, just a few years later, as a student at the Royal Manchester College of Music, my Music of the Spheres("a bucolic tone poem for French horn and orchestra") had its premiere. It launched me onto the international stage, hence my old school wanting to honour me — no doubt hoping to boost fundraising and recruitment.

Of course, to this day, no one really knows what my tone poem was trying to evoke. I'd decided against my original title, Ars Musica, which, I thought, was a bit of a giveaway. Who wants to be branded a fart fetishist?

Flatus is certainly a neglected topic in the arts. Okay, there's jokes in Rabelais and Shakespeare, but few are sympathetic, James Joyce being the exception, praising his wife and muse, Nora Barnacle, for her "long windy ones" and "big fat fellows." Joyce even has a collection of verse — not much read — called Chamber Music, which, for me, evokes the poetry of the Water Closet. I've set a few of these verses to music, but no critic has yet made the connection with Music of the Spheres.

Isn't that what music's about, though? All art, in fact. Capturing the everyday and turning it into something sublime. Showing the listener that, out of our fragile flesh, something immortal emerges. Almost against our will, we're transported by it.

***

After I finished cleaning the hall, I went straight to Salford General. Nowadays I can visit Tony whenever I want. Almost like one of the staff, I am. I can even make myself a brew.

I couldn't get over seeing that young upstart down at school, though I know he was a pupil there some twenty-five … thirty years ago? Today he was all dressed up in his finery. Dr Robert Martin-Evans, indeed! Who'd have seen that coming? Plain Bobby Evans he was back then.

He didn't even recognise me. I know I'm no bombshell anymore, but still. The amount of time he used to spend gawping, you'd think something would have stuck! Ogling me round every corner, he was. Never felt safe with him around.

His parents, though, were lovely. Old couple, I always thought, to have such a youngster. It must be ten years or so since they moved into sheltered housing. Best neighbours we ever had — Bobby excepted!

I couldn't shake him off. Didn't seem to have no friends. Always on his own, he was, carrying one of his flutes or whistles. Not natural for a lad! There were several times Tony came to his rescue after seeing him bullied. But what did the lad expect, waltzing home in his school uniform, playing that poncy music? Never got no thanks for it, neither, didn't Tony. The lad seemed to think himself special, worth protecting.

A strange one, popping up in the most peculiar places — from behind the bins or in his dad's vegetable patch, like some exotic bloom! How his dad used to love that little patch of earth. George — real gent he was! Mind you, both he and Gladys were lovely. Don't know what happened with Bobby! George used to give us carrots, peas and stuff — anything he'd a glut of. And occasionally, he'd present me with a bunch of flowers.

Bobby, though, was creepy, especially given my condition. Thought I'd be able to relax when we moved into our council house, especially having our own garden. But no. His lordship was always lurking. Bad enough inheriting the family curse —IBS — without him sniggering at every bit of wind you passed. I'm sure he used to imitate me on that flute he was forever tootling. Cheeky young sod!

And when I hung out my washing, there he'd be, up in his room, drooling over my smalls. I lost some of my best things off that line. I'm sure it was him. Of course, he denied all knowledge. I should have confronted him just now in the school hall, shouldn't I? That would have been a laugh. What would the Head have made of that? Respected old boy, my backside! Not that Bobby was too different from many of the lads back then, I suppose. I'd been chased by 'em since I was about ten. Like a pack of dogs, they were. Couldn't keep their paws off you. Only after one thing, dirty lot!

That is, until they heard me. Not the sort of noise they expected to come from your knickers. Didn't fancy me then, did they? Rolling round with laughter, they'd be, or holding their noses, as if the poor innocents never passed wind in their lives!

There were exceptions, I suppose, but none like Tony. Made for each other, we were, with our ropey organs. In fact, it was in Salford General that we first got talking. That's when we discovered what we had in common. What's tragic is, that hospital might also be the last place I'll ever see Tony. Still, we've tried to make every day count, haven't we?

***

Betts was in this evening again. She's a star. Mind you, I think she knows it's curtains, bless her. She's a good 'un. Perhaps the doctors have had a word. "His days are numbered," I can just hear them saying. Like to keep it vague, they do. Never call a spade a spade. What would I have done without Betts? It's been a difficult sort of life, but she's made it worthwhile. My mates couldn't believe it when they discovered I was going out with Bombshell Betty. We'd all lusted after her, but here was me, actually dating her. The lads with their Charles Atlas figures would look at me, my six-pack more like a beer-barrel, and gasp in disbelief: "Betty Thomas," they'd say, "going out with … you?" Of course, they eventually got to know why. Changed their tune then, didn't they? Me and Betty were just a couple of spazzes, weren't we? Soiled goods — just right for each other! Her with her IBS and me with hepatitis.

Chronic hepatitis B. Caught it from me dad, didn't I, who was out in Korea. It finished him off, too. Treatment's better nowadays but, even so, my days are numbered, as the doctors like to say. My liver's so distended and scarred they can do nothing more. Cirrhosis is what it is, although I don't like the word. People always think you're some sad boozer. But I've hardly touched a drop, despite all the pints the lads used to line up. Weak shandy is all I supped. It was darts took me to The Red Lion, little else.

So, there we both were, misfits, sitting alongside one other in hospital awaiting our treatments, and we got talking. Couldn't believe my luck. And what's a bit of wind, anyway, or flatulence, as the doctors like to call it? Always dress things up do the doctors. Whatever you call it, I know our Betts suffered something chronic. Not just the pain — though that's bad enough. I'm talking psychologically, cos she was such a beauty. I mean, if no one had drooled over her in the first please, it wouldn't have mattered so much. But there she was, drop-dead gorgeous …

Without Betts, I'd have had a sorry little life, that's for sure. It's just a shame we never had kids. We were both mad for 'em, but it didn't seem fair, given what we'd suffered. God knows what sort of creatures our messed-up bodies would have produced. Betts never forgave her own mother for that.

And speaking of messed-up, Betts told me that she'd seen our old neighbours' kid, Bobby. Lovely couple were George and Gladys, but what a mixed-up item he was! Fancy running into him after all these years! I used to worry about Betts being in the garden with him on the loose. Used to pinch her underwear off the line, he did. And more than a few times I caught him playing with himself in the vegetable patch. Just polishing my pipe, he'd say. Yeah! He was another one for the roundabout talk.

Joking aside, the lad did spend an awful lot of time playing those instruments of his. Artsy-fartsy stuff it was. Not the sort of thing you could hum along to! They played some of it on Radio Salford, earlier. I wouldn't have had a clue who it was if Betty hadn't tipped me off. Dr Robert Martin-Evans, indeed! It's not the stuff you usually hear, and you could tell that the DJ, Bradley Madden, wasn't impressed either, even if Bobby was a local lad made good. Obviously, the boy's making the most of his fleeting return to his roots. I wonder if he's been to see his folks, though? … if they're still around.

After Bradley had played Bobby's piece, he let slip that the lad originally called it "Ars Musica." Bradley milked that for a few jokes, I can tell you! I was with him. A bigger load of shite only comes out of elephants' backsides!

Not that I listened that closely. I found myself transported back to our first years in that house. My gorgeous Betts! How she loved that garden, waltzing round it in the sunshine, marking time with her dandelion clocks. She loved them. I couldn't bear to pull 'em up. Perhaps, even then, blowing away those seeds, she knew something about how fleeting and fragile it all is.

So, I can't say I paid much attention to Dr Bobby and his arsy-fartsy music. I was back in our past, savouring our magic moments together.

David Rudd

Susan Dwyer

Earnest Correspondence

October 5

Dearest Earnest,

I remain optimistic despite the fact that all the glass broke yesterday. A sharp diagonal crack across the window at the foot of the bed just as I awoke, and then another through my glass on the nightstand. I watched the water begin to pool and roll toward your book, whose pages absorbed the wetness, slowly and at their own pace. Your words, my dear, appear to have imparted a certain dignity — even *gravitas* — to that paper. It was clear there would be no hurry.

After a while, I arose and pulled my green robe about myself in, what I confess, was a somewhat slovenly fashion and made my way downstairs. Passing the grandfather clock in the hall, I spotted a nick in its face. In the kitchen, every single glass on the shelf next to the cooker had shattered into its own hillock of sparkling despair. And then I heard the chandelier in the dining room begin to rattle. Why the suspense? Both it and I knew what was to happen next. The trembling, well, it was just unnecessary. Impolite. Like Daddy and his belt, you'll recall. Stroking it softly its whole length. The way he'd look at you with such a delight of anticipation. *Just get on with it*, I always thought. M.

October 23

Dearest Earnest,

Today it was the cows, whining about their blankets. It seems they do not care for the scented soap — heavenly lavender — I have been using to clean them. Quite sensitive creatures. But what, really, do they have to complain about. They have their grass and dips in the ground and plenty of water. I have put away my arrows, the dogs are no longer allowed near them, and, of course, they have their blankets! Several, in fact, as I like to change up and according to the seasons. M.

November 18

Dearest Earnest,

The bees persist. In the pillows. In the rabbit hutches. What shall I do? Mrs. S. is of no help whatsoever! Muddling along in her apron, all smiles but with that sneaky eye I know you know. In general, the pillows, I don't mind so much. And I do like the bees. They sometimes make a fuzzy moving mass on my arm when I am dozing, as I do so often now. Several times this week I've woken up — well, 'come to' — in a chair in the parlor, not having a clue where I am. I think the bees sense the departure of identity and get settled in. I'm sorry that this stiff, dry body deceives them into thinking that there might be some sustenance here.

November 3

Dearest Earnest,

I like the black stars best. There's a sort of reliability to them, which, as we know, is quite different from predictability. (Cruelty comes in endless forms most cruel.) The black stars beckon. They make no excuses. I like the way they press their backs against alley walls. Observe silently. Bear what they see. Share rarely. What use is conversation to a black star? Maybe, do you think, it's that they don't want to talk back?

Have the black stars been with you too, Earnest? Or have you not yet returned from the tour? I hope you took your brown coat; the one with the really deep pockets. The one with the small stain on the left, at the back, close to the seam.

The black stars are cold, which I appreciate. As I said, no excuses. M.

December 2

Dearest Earnest,

How are your ankles? Last evening I saw old Thomas Corbett, Esq. at some interminable community meeting and he asked. I feigned ignorance, not wanting to extend any time talking with him (given the history) and, of course, to protect your dignity. How could he, of all people, have known? Who else might? Oh dear, this will have you fretting. Do not fear that anyone will discover the culprit, or what remains of him. Your secrets are safe with me. Your secrets are my secrets, and mine yours. The world is a better place without him. Enough. M.

December 15

Dearest Earnest,

It gives me much comfort to write to you on these cold mornings when I awake screaming from my latest nightmare. I would be less afraid, and less apt to scream, if visited at four o'clock by an actual mare. But that is not going to happen. A mare I have already, in any event, and she is mostly a day mare to me, since I am never at the farm at night. What does she do? Whom does she terrify? And if there is no one else to scare, does she stand wide-eyed and terrified herself, flank pressed up against the stone wall? (Along with the black stars?) M.

December 23

Dearest Earnest,

Should I get a snake, do you think? No, no, before you flinch, I am not concerned about the mice. Those, dear one, have been taken care of in ways you should not bother your pretty old skull with. Rather, my interest in the snake (or maybe snakes?) has to do with unwanted guests of the human variety. It's all well and good to have people over for tea. They can, on occasion, be mildly amusing. I am thinking of Connie Britton — pig farmer and post mistress. Although she brings the odor of her beasts with her and her nails are always dirty, I do like — well, shall we say, I momentarily have positive dispositions towards — her or towards her forthrightness. Having ventured bravely into the Post Office once last year, I understand that forthrightness is quite the attitude in demand. How else could one possibly survive a day there? I mean, what is the point of wondering about the weather, when all that is needed is an exchange of some coins for a stamp?

So, yes, Connie has learned to be direct. Do you think the pigs appreciate it? Does she, I wonder, tell them, "Well, pig, today is your day for the axe. Best to say your goodbyes over the morning slop. For death is certain, though it will be quick!" I think if I were to be slaughtered, I should want to know about it just like this. Not unkindly, but with a certainty that embodies a peculiar comfort of its own. Death ought not be a nasty surprise. M.

January 7

Dearest Earnest,

Cast your mind back to Maud. Oh, I know it will seem painful. But, dear one, do it for me, please? Do you remember the corpse face, the wide staring eyes? But more than that, the perfect blackness of the open mouth? The mouth open in death in a way that utterly belied its living manifestation. Maud of the pouts, of the — what are they called? — the *moués*, of disappointment, disapproval, of dyspepsia. We never really knew, did we? Maud was always tight-lipped. But still managed volubility. That was what set her apart. In silence, she condemned and accused and always won. And then dead, she was tight-lipped no more. She was not exactly agape, for she was in awe of nothing. Not even of her own formidable self. M.

January 19

Dearest Earnest,

In one of the dusty cardboard boxes you left, I came across a bespoke Bunny suit. Yes, you know what I mean. One of those corseted, satiny, strapless leotard affairs to be worn with fishnet stockings, high heels and a preposterous set of ears. I never found the tuft of a tail preposterous at all. Indeed, if one is to be about in the world — well, one's place of work, I should say — in a strapless leotard, the tail strikes me as an acceptable if not, indeed, an entirely appropriate accessory. Who made this suit for whom? This question interests me less than the experience of the one wearing it. Was it comfortable? Could she sit on her tail? Or was she to be the type of bunny always required to be reared up? Nose twitching like my rabbits here under the shed, who eat my coriander. M.

January 31

Dearest Earnest,

If it would not occasion a snide look from you, I would ask your advice about this thin place. Which I have just done! The depths of winter are such a solace to me. I love to lie in bed, with my yellow covers and watch the pale grey-pink dawn emerge. M.

February 3

Dearest Earnest,

Whence this wind? Damned fields. So long ago. So tufted treacherous. Despaired, didn't we? Wet socks and tearing eyes. And all for what? We thought the quest so important then. I still have the envelope, now impossible to read, and the stamp that is only half there. It is like a flap of soft flesh and just as disgusting to me. Why do you make me keep it? And why do I? And why, oh why, on this date each year, do I dutifully assure you of my obedience? Obedience! Now there's a fine word for it. M.

February 29

Dearest Earnest,

Tell me again of the woods. Not what happened, but where things occurred. The trees. The small animals. The sky. How it smelled. The ground beneath your feet. How your hair was dampened by the mist. I doubt I shall ever tire of the tale. But, again, dear one, it is the 'where' I love the most. I hear the snap of twigs. The shuffling of the leaves. The drip, drip, drip of the condensing fog. Always fog then, wasn't there? Things were always 'looming'. Do remember Mrs. Loomis. So aptly named! The way she would emerge, across the gravel, in those sinister skirts and low brown shoes. Such impossibly small feet for all that stood above. And the dainty ankles. Well, yes, she loomed the largest.

What was it, do you think, she brought with her? It wasn't just the smell of town. Or the cat hairs. Whatever it was, we all felt it. But she had the good grace to take it with her when she left. Or, perhaps, she had no say in the matter. Perhaps what came across the gravel, what loomed towards us all, brought Mrs. Loomis herself. So, it was her, substantially hipped though she was, that was the thing brought along. M.

March 5

Dearest Earnest,

The rain is alive this morning. A million writhing rain creatures roiling the air and moiling the view. I awoke breathing water. It will not stop and I am feeling as though I am myself running down panes and pooling the gutters. It is not an altogether unpleasant feeling. However, it does require attention.

So often now, dear one, I find I must *add attention* to the smallest things. I give myself instructions and, sometimes, even the most ridiculous exhortations, out loud, as if I were a squad of muddy-kneed boys on the field. All this is tiring. I was amused at first by the growing habit of narrating tea-making and moving up and down the stairs. But now, I fear, it is not amusing at all. It is, like the rain today, deadly serious. Will I die mid-sentence? Mid cheer? Mid encouraging? How sad that might be. M.

Susan Dywer

Lucy Brighton

Megalodon, (*Carcharocles megalodon*), member of an extinct species of megatooth shark.

That summer, I learned everything there was to know about Megalodons. I sat, cross-legged in the stiff-backed chair beside your bed, with a book from the library balanced between my knees and I studied it while Mum talked to you like a baby, with all the *there theres*.

The Megalodon is the largest fish that ever lived.

I told you the facts from the book when Mum went to get food or coffee or to cry in the corridor. Sometimes you nodded a little, but your eyes didn't stay on me. They rolled about searching for imaginary devils on the ceiling. *That's just the medication*, Mum said, *He knows monsters aren't real.*

Megalodons possessed an estimated 276 teeth.

Look, I said, holding the glossy pictures of gaping fossilized jaws over your head. Your mouth had grown in that bed. Your teeth too big for your face, the skin like tissue paper about your bones.

The Megalodon was an apex predator.

Can you imagine? I asked, *everything else in the sea feared them. They would even eat whales and dolphins. Nothing was safe from the Megalodon!* You were scared, you mumbled in fits of sleep about fire and damnation. Mum said it was *catholic indoctrination*. I didn't know what she meant.

The Megalodon was estimated to be between 14.2–20.3 metres.

Mum said I was over a metre tall. *That means the Meg would be 20 times bigger than me*, I told you, laying on the hospital floor trying to imagine ten of me in front and ten behind. *That's huge.* Mum had found me stretched out and told me to get up, that the floor was dirty. It didn't look dirty. Everything was shiny and clean because you couldn't *afford to come in contact with any germs*.

The Megalodon went extinct approximately 2.5 million years ago.

That's a long time ago, I told you, dabbing your cracked lips with the small, wet sponge on a stick. When I was done, you smacked them together and reached out to touch my face. It made me flinch and I know it shouldn't have, that you were still you. Your fingers were the texture of wood bark. Your chest rattled as you sucked in a deep breath.

"I love you," you said in a phlegmy voice.

The megalodon is thought to be an ancestor of the great white shark.

If you were a Meg, that would make me a great white, I told you as I watched you fade out of existence like they had done all those millennia ago. Like them, you couldn't survive the changes. For them, the cooling of the ocean, the shifting of the food chain. For you, the mutations of your cells, your DNA recoding. That summer, I learned everything there was to know about Megalodons.

Lucy Brighton

Fiona Scott-Barrett

Have you seen the onion man?

The Onion Johnnies came over from Brittany every December, wheeling their black bicycles up the streets of our hilly city, strings of onions hanging from the handlebars. My mother liked to invite them in and practise her French on them before buying a rope of pink-tinged onions that would see us through most of the winter.

The year I was four, she made her customary offer of a small nip of whisky to the Onion Johnny, but this one was young, more a boy than a man, and he declined. So, she showed him our Christmas tree and invited him to choose a chocolate decoration off it. As every year, we had hung the glass decorations that came out of an old cardboard box stuffed with yellowing tissue paper to protect them. As every year, one or two, friable with age, had broken as we handled them. The resulting gaps on the tree were filled with foil-wrapped chocolate decorations.

Mum was chatting in French and pointing out the edible decorations when the phone rang. She excused herself and went into the hall to answer it, leaving the Breton boy and me perusing the tree. His hand reached out towards a shiny toadstool, its red and white cap reflecting the glinting fairy lights.

I was a shy child, and my voice came out as a squeak. "Not that one," I said. "It's glass, not chocolate."

The boy looked confused.

"It's not chocolate," I squeaked again.

He smiled and nodded at me, plucked the decoration from the tree and with great deliberation bit off the cap of the toadstool and crunched it slowly.

When my mother returned, he was still crewing doggedly, oblivious to the trail of blood dripping from the corner of his mouth onto his black jersey.

"None of this happened," my mother said, and packed me off to bed far too early. For three weeks I was banned from entering the guest bedroom. Christmas lunch was to be different that year, mother told me. Not turkey, but a delicious leg of lamb, cooked with plenty of onions.

When the day came, our house was full of the smell of onions and roasting flesh. Mum was enthusiastic about her new dish and urged as all to have seconds, but I did not. I thought it was rather stringy.

George R. Justice

Jo-Jo

Aside from the occasional iguana, emerald and iridescent and upwards to six feet long, the balminess of December in Boca Raton makes my mantra (*shorts, t-shirts and sandals forever*) all the more palpable, and my relocation to it all the more obvious. From the convergence of Bentley's and BMW's to the mix of day spas and pool boys, Boca Raton is sophistication leveraged in the awe of insider trading and the abhorrence of loose skin, and all reminiscent of the Jersey shore in mid-July. And though I am heightened by its wellbeing and the free flow of its cash reserves, there is a festering sore. I speak here of Jo-Jo, a shambling, half-albino rat who lives under my hot tub, and does so in spite of my zip code.

Jo-Jo is a hyphenated amalgamation of the name Josiah Johnson: my eighth grade Phys-Ed teacher who whipped my bare legs with the chain from his whistle as I ran laps around the gym, or rather when I didn't run them fast enough. He was also the brother-in-law of school superintendent Millard Mullins and poster child for the stink-arm of nepotism. But when his enormous belly-over-the-belt physic and raspy '*please-get-me-to-a-ventilator*' inhalations turned his pasty flesh to crimson and his heart to a syncopating time bomb, the better part of Millard Mullins opted in favor of Mr. Johnson going from Phys-Ed teacher to driving the school bus. Lovely. But then someone was clever enough to say that Josiah's downgrade wasn't so much about politics as it was about pasta. Without making too much of it, I believed, as did Hess Henrik, my head-tattooed locker partner, that it was the rumors about Mr. Johnson's clown-sized boxer shorts and his teeny-tiny bursts of Prozac intolerance that worked to unseat him and further elevate the lard in his flanks. Nothing of the kind could be said about Jo-Jo, although, given his thickset, a point could be made for the pasta.

At first glance, Jo-Jo conjured the notion of genuine sin: reliable and dependable evil somewhere on the level of *The Joker* in the creep and shadows of Gotham. His very fur, a faux-hoarfrost of lice and trans fats, seemed to congeal in the fair light of Boca's marshmallow moon. At first I thought him harmless enough, little more than, say, an extra from *Willard*. Later, I thought better of it when he gnawed away the brass ball valve on my hot tub's cold water line. It was then that things began to change.

Right from the beginning, when we first locked eyes, my only thought was to *get* him. Being from the hills of Kentucky, that's what we do: we *get* things before they *get* us. As logic would dictate, I baited a traditional trap (the old standard spring-loaded, cock-at-the-risk-of-losing-everything-from-nose-to-knuckles, contraption) with a bite-sized chuck of imported Havarti, an estimable hors d'oeuvre by any standard. To my amazement, Jo-Jo was adroit enough to trip the trap without any obvious repercussions then slip back into the night, the lingering aroma of Havarti in his wake. That was late September, and though loathe to admit it, I was somewhat bemused by Jo-Jo's inventiveness, putting it right up there with the shamanisms of devil worshipping shoe salesmen from Ohio. So, like anyone from a long line of trappers and accustomed to the occasional disappointment of having no meat for the table, I reloaded the trap. Over and again. Night after night. Each time with the same results, and each time growing a wee bit more unsure of the glue meant to hold me together. Was Jo-Jo proving to be higher in the food chain than I cared to admit? — more refined in the ways of survival? —more in tune to that smooth dark river that runs through us all and, God forbid, somehow connects us?

In the days that followed, inclination steered me back to that first semester of junior college when I was supposed to read Joseph Conrad's *The Heart of Darkness*, but never did. Had I missed out? —had I shortchanged myself of some valuable lesson pertaining to the life and death struggle of man vs. things deceitfully conceived and ill mannered? —things such as Jo-Jo? Was there something beyond the table of Cliff Notes that had eluded me to its possibilities? Aside from its title, *Heart of Darkness*, an appellation right away reflective of my mood, there seemed to be nothing beyond the mishmash of ethos and pathos that I could identify; little outside the camphoric wheezing about concurrent themes and motifs and such. It seemed so unfair that I be left wondering about my dereliction of responsibilities, my slight to academia, and how it may have left me unprepared for the ilks of nature. But then it didn't take much to recognize the out-and-out squalor Jo-Jo imposed on Boca's jeweled celebrity. He was, outright, a patent reminder of why we kept ourselves gated; a symbolic snag to our sheened catamarans and thousand-count, hand-brushed cottons.

The struggle for life and death is too often an overlooked theme for the star-studded nights of Boca Raton. That being the case, however, a midnight landscape with vagaries too impolite for either silk or senses is where Jo-Jo and I ultimately found ourselves, and where we, juxtaposed far from the nuances of make believe and a city postured in paradise, would draw the line in Boca's very powdery, hourglass sand.

In the lenient autumn days that followed, I bought a Have-A-Heart trap and baited it with (hold on) peanut butter. HA! The only thing left was to wait for daylight and the drive into the everglades to set him loose. But then I never counted on him rolling the damned thing onto its side (like one would tip a cow I suppose), tripping its doors and allowing unrestricted access. I stood there in the soft hue of Boca's early light with a sense that my freedom, even my free will, was being jackhammered into a diaphanous pulp. An ocean breeze, scented and even-handed, stirred the few remaining hairs on my head and signaled me that I was not alone; that Jo-Jo's teensy little misfit eyes were, at that very moment, lurking somewhere in the Trumpet Creeper, sizing me up for yet another round.

Alright! Enough already! My only thought: You mess with the bull, you get the horn!" And with that, I marched straight to the garage and my stash of tent pegs, coat hangers and zip ties: everything I needed to anchor this Have-A-Heart trap into a lasting upright position. NO MORE TIPPING, UPENDING, OR DERAILING! The sheriff was back in town and the hunt now elevated to high alert. The trap, lavishly baited with the sweet goo of (get this) honey and chocolate chips, now lazed in the watery thickets of lobelia. My pursuit had gained momentum, been elevated to code red. A lasting salvo was at hand. What a blessed sleep I could count on just knowing that this was Jo-Jo's last night in my garden.

Dawn broke with the fragrance of dew and salt spray from the Atlantic coaxing Boca into my every pore. I was awake with its first breath and the fullness of its genesis, and with only one thing on my mind: get Jo-Jo and get him into the backwaters far from Boca.

I bypassed breakfast, of course, and headed straight for the prize. But then the prize proved to be more of a *sur*prise. The Have-A-Heart trap was upright, in place, intact, even tripped—the honey and chocolate chips gone—but no Jo-Jo. Where in the name of Abraham, Isaac and Jacob was Jo-Jo? I stood there, imported silk pajamas draped just-so to the tops of my hand-stitched Italian slippers, locked into the idea that I was somehow Jo-Jo's plaything; and that he was, in total, unappreciative that the Have-A-Heart trap was meant to be sympathetic—a compassionate alternative to its spring loaded cousin. Clearly, he was powerless to say 'no thank you' to what was meant as a kindness. Okay! Deep breaths! Deep-deep breaths.

Cavernous funk, menacing and all-pervading, was never anymore prevalent, equivalent in a very fundamental way to the sound of cow chips being flung against a barndoor. My head hurt, throbbed actually, and could only conclude that Divine Providence had sided with Jo-Jo, not an altogether groundless assumption seeing as how he had obviously been genetically advantaged with the finer requisites of how to stay alive. As for me, I remained inked in angst what with the neighbors smirking and going on about me mucking about with a rat.

But just as providence was working to animate Jo-Jo, fate was working to enliven me. What one might conclude as a tacit turn of kismet, came at me with a new level of awareness, one spawned only by a mercurial need to reach beyond the credos of decency; an awareness that connected me to the lowest levels of self and the essentials of urgency, an idea whose time had come. *ZING! POW!* … just like that … and then … calmness, a sense of persuasion as blissful as the soft indigo in Boca's high-noon sky. I knew in an instant, in the shade and reverence of Royal palms, what had to be done: *glue trap!* I would lay into Jo-Jo with the certitude of *glue.* Oh, Villainy!

I really had no intentions of stooping to the use of a *glue trap*, but here I was between a rock and a sharp place. What was I to do? Ignore my most basic instincts? I don't think so. And so it was: the dreaded glue trap and its repute as the toller of bells. When all else fails, one understandably brings in the heavy equipment: elite units and their barrage of no-nonsense. In my case, it was *glue traps*!

It was not an easy night, tossing and turning, knowing that Jo-Jo's time had finally come. Funny how I could derive such simple pleasure from the fact that I was *man*, the top of the food chain, washed in reason and in whom God had given dominion over the earth and all therein. In the end, lowly little things like Jo-Jo had about as much chance as a raindrop in a forest fire. But then if Jo-Jo was going to be truly gotten, it only stood to reason that it would have to be done with a degree of cunning. But then despite the certainty of the glue trap, Jo-Jo would first have to be *lured, drawn in*. I had to appeal to his baser self, his *something for nothing indulgence,* something I knew was the bigger part of him.

So, on the eve of my revelation, I set out globs of bait (Velveeta with sprinklings of Limburger) on black pieces of construction paper the same size and color as the glue traps. Let him come and eat, let him see that there's nothing to fear. I did and he did. He came, he saw, he ate. Oh, cunning!

On night two, I simply replicated what I did on night one, this time with a black odorless glue trap instead of construction paper. The rest? Victory, of course! … Wellllllllll … not entirely!

Morning came as it always did to the garden wonder of Boca Raton and, to my amazement, nothing had been disturbed, moved or eaten. The blend of Velveeta and Limburger sat as it had the night before, only now looking as lost and forlorn as the glue paper itself. Where was the justice? —the fulfillment of revenge? —and where was Jo-Jo? Although gone from sight, I was never more sure that he was, at that very minute, secreted away in some deep dank hole snickering inaudibly. But it was in that moment of sureness that I was able to let it go, rather let *him* go. The rest of the day ebbed and flowed in a mauve and periwinkle haze so distinctive of Boca. But as the sun dipped behind a fuchsia and magenta colored horizon, I was left only with the wonder of '*Where do I go from here?*'

Jo-Jo became no less than an enigma in the days that followed. Had he gotten braver? —gone over the wall? —expanded his territory? I was almost insulted thinking he had. At times and in fits of fantasy, I could see him squinty-eyed and laughing, reliving the outrageous sequence of our skirmishes. But I was mollified in large part by my belief that his exodus meant that he had finally run out of tricks, and that his continuing to hang around would ultimately reduce his chances of longevity. Add to that Boca's boundless seasonal softness, its penchant for all that glittered, all that was glossed and tanned, and I waxed content knowing that I had in some small way prevailed, come out on top, although by default.

***

It was early dawn in late January, when Venus beamed like a solitary diamond and my footsteps were lost in the frenzy of grackles, that I saw Jo-Jo for the final time: flat, and in the likeness of an old shoe steamrolled (three? —four times?) and with a look of peace stamped forever on his face. His hands were together, fashioned in prayer … his final gesture I guessed. I recognized him straightaway by the colorless, albino blob on his hindquarter, that unmistakable mark of the devil. For the first time he appeared somber, apologetic, even poetic. But they were gestures far too late. I was unmoved.

Had Jo-Jo, sometime during the night, stumbled off course? —reeled and gasped a final time from a dose of something lethal? Little wonder the grackles only circled, only came so close. My guess was that he upended just before one of the sub-division's SUV's molded him to its carefully crafted, terracotta pavers. Serendipity, that cold and indifferent jot of fate, had, in a flash, sounded out Taps for ole Jo-Jo and his dismaying bag of tricks.

Even though there was a sense of indulgence seeing him there, flattened to paper-thin and stiff as rawhide, there was the lingering thought that he had had the last laugh, outsmarted my bank of testosterone and logic alike. I can't say as I was humbled by it, only somewhat relieved that I had ultimately not been his executioner. And, too, there was the feeling of forfeiture—however slight—the kind that comes with the loss of a foe so formidable and knowing that I would be denied another chance to settle the score.

It's hard to say what lay at the core of Jo-Jo's demise and his final encounter with oncoming traffic. If indeed it was poison, I don't know that it would have ever been my choice, only because of its unpredictability—him dying and rotting under my hot tub as the foulest of possibilities. All told, and without even the hint of acrimony, I left him there, free of pain and within the agitation of blackbirds. The morning, otherwise, passed without incident, none of it, though, as apt and deft as my footsteps going away, or as bracing as the backdrop of bougainvillea and the ocean breeze stirring high in the palms.

It was only minutes before the first rays of Boca's seamless sun went about erasing all thoughts of Jo-Jo and warming me once again to the prisms of its light.

George R. Justice

From the Editors

Matthew's Twin: The spirit of medieval vengeance made flesh

Belfast Ghosts: Standalone Book 3 of 3

A medieval Scottish soldier.
An Anglo-Irish witch.
A seven hundred year plot for revenge.

Around the time Matthew began having crippling stomach pains, he began witnessing visions of a past-life involving a Scottish soldier during Edward Bruce's invasion of Ireland, an Anglo-Irish defender of Carrickfergus Castle and a local witch with a bloodthirsty agenda. When medieval mercenary and vengeful witch performed a necromantic ritual to help the Scottish conquest succeed, Matthew began to learn more about his connection with medieval Ulster.

After an operation to remove what he thought to be a tumour from his stomach, a mysterious man arrived to cause chaos in Matthew's life. What did the strange - yet familiar - man have to do with him? Why did malign forces from a dark, medieval past want to cause harm? Was there any way for Matthew to learn about a seven hundred year injustice before the ghosts came to wreak vengeance on him in the present?

Available for FREE on Kindle Unlimited and in paperback and hardcover from Amazon, Barnes & Noble, Foyles, Waterstones and more:

The Blue Man: A haunted friendship across the decades

Belfast Ghosts Series: Standalone Book 1 of 3

Chill with a Book Premier Readers' Award and Book of the Month winner, February 2023

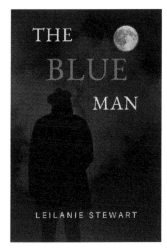

Two best friends. An urban legend. A sinister curse.

Twenty years ago teenage friends, Megan and Sabrina, destroyed their friendship after learning the terrifying Irish urban legend of the Blue Man and unleashing a sinister force into their lives. Now, as mothers-to-be, they reunite once more to confront the horror and trauma. Could they finally bury the past and change the fate of their families?

Available for FREE on Kindle Unlimited, and in paperback and hardcover from Amazon, Barnes & Noble, Waterstones and more.

The Fairy Lights: The ghost of Christmas that never was

Belfast Ghosts Series: Standalone Book 2 of 3

When Aisling moves into an old Edwardian house, she soon realises her student digs are haunted by a ghost known locally as Jimbo. As yuletide approaches, she uses the fairy lights to attract Jimbo and with the help of a local psychic and friends from her university course, seeks to uncover dark, buried truths. But what will the spirit world reveal about her own past?

Available for FREE from Kindle Unlimited and in paperback and hardcover from Amazon, Barnes & Noble, Foyles, Waterstones and more.

The Buddha's Bone: A dark psychological journey to find light

She was in Japan to teach English. She'd soon discover the darker side of travelling alone.

Kimberly Thatcher was a Londoner who set off to teach English in Japan on a one year contract. After escaping her abusive boyfriend back in London, she soon found herself pursued by a colleague – with even more sinister intentions than her ex. Kimberly would soon learn the darker nature of her relationships, forcing her on a soul-searching journey through darkness to find the light. What happened when you looked into the abyss?

Available for FREE from Kindle Unlimited and in paperback and hardcover from Amazon, Barnes & Noble, Foyles, Waterstones and more.

Diabolical Dreamscapes: Strange and macabre short stories

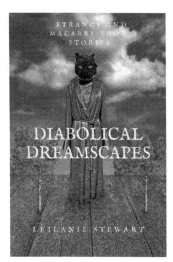

Reader beware! From the hallucinatory imagination of Leilanie Stewart, author of award-winning ghost horror novel, The Blue Man, comes twenty-one previously published short stories and flash fiction, now entombed between the covers of a new darkly themed collection.

What you are about to read will befuddle your mind, addle your brain, render you into a delirium from which you may not recover. These twenty-one tales feature disturbing creations from a strange and surreal imagination and are not for the faint-hearted. May you tread with caution, for once you read them, you cannot un-read them.

Available for FREE from Kindle Unlimited and in paperback and hardcover from Amazon, Barnes & Noble, Foyles, Waterstones and more.

A Model Archaeologist

Archaeologist by day, glamour model by night.

These 80 poems playfully explore the uncertainties of an archaeology graduate entering the workforce in an uncertain economic climate. *A Model Archaeologist* comprises a series of lyrical anecdotes using poetic license to turn lemons into lemonade. The collection can at times be deceptively simple, show subtle humour and have a self-deprecating edge of satire, reflecting the naiveté of youth.

Available for FREE on Kindle Unlimited and in hardcover from Amazon, Foyles and Waterstones.

The Redundancy of Tautology

Leilanie Stewart's third poetry collection comprises 80 acerbic poems exploring the existential horror of eternal recurrence through everyday objects, situations and places.

Or if you like, the endless occurrence of day-to-day things, happenings and locations.

Available for FREE on Kindle Unlimited and in paperback from Amazon, Barnes & Noble and more.

Mastered Thesis

Joseph Robert's collection from Cyberwit comprises 30 pieces of poems and prose; an irreverent and light-spleened take on the state-funded factory.

Available in paperback from Amazon, Barnes & Noble and more.

Brexit Brokeshit

A collection of poetry and prose on the subject of Brexit, its causes, personalities and conflicts. A righteous statement on the virtues of political impotence, "I'm not racist but…" political figures and, oh, to hell with all of it…

Available for FREE on Kindle Unlimited and in paperback from Amazon, Barnes & Noble and more.

Visit Joseph Robert's Amazon author page for all books:

https://www.amazon.com/Joseph-Robert/e/B09HXL2QFD/

AUTHOR BIOS

Mary Anne Abdo is an emergent writer of poetry. With a background in freelance journalism. She uses her poetry as a source of creative expression. That reflects the many faucets of what it means to be human living in these modern times. Mary Anne has a passion for art, culture and literature. She graduated Magna Cum Laude from Luzerne County Community College with a degree in Human Services. She has been featured in The Edge of Humanity Magazine, The Skeptics Kaddish The Avocet, Calla Press, Moonstone Press, Local Gems Press, and Studio B Poetry Anthology 2022-2023. A Museum of Prayer second place prizewinner for her photography and prose of a Mary's Garden July 2022. Her first collaborative children's book Creative Gems Volume 2 and Bindweed Magazine 2022-2023. She has made regular appearances on Rattlecast podcast. Her first poetry book Fractured Lollipop Poems of Brokenness Health and Hope is on Amazon You may check out her work on: Facebook Mary Anne Abdo/author WordPress https://bluestainedglass.wordpress.com Instagram https://www.instagram.com/maryanne.abdo/

L. Sydney Abel is an author of psychological fiction and poetry. He was born and raised in Kingston upon Hull, England. His novel *12:07 The Sleeping* is based on personal experience of sleep paralysis and his forthcoming book *The Soul Spook* continues this theme. He has also written and illustrated several children's books and a Y/A novel *Timothy Other: The boy who climbed Marzipan Mountain*, the first in a series of three.
Poetry is his personal escape in his book of emotive words *Tongue is a Fire* and the upcoming *One ASYLUM*.

Social Media:
https://theslider58.wixsite.com/lsydneyabel
https://www.lsydneyabelbooks.com/
https://theslider58.wixsite.com/lsydneyabelpoet

Ed Ahern resumed writing after forty odd years in foreign intelligence and international sales. He's had four hundred fifty stories and poems published so far, and seven books. Ed works the other side of writing at Bewildering Stories, where he manages a posse of eight review editors. He's also lead editor at The Scribes Micro Fiction magazine.
https://www.twitter.com/bottomstripper
https://www.facebook.com/EdAhern73/?ref=bookmarks
https://www.instagram.com/edwardahern1860/

Jim Bates lives in a small town west of Minneapolis, Minnesota. He loves to write! His stories and poems have appeared in nearly five hundred online and print publications. He is the author of nine collections of short stories, two novels, two novellas, one collection of haiku poems, and one collection of poetry. Check out his blog at: www.theviewfromlonglake.wordpress.com.

Gary Beck has spent most of his adult life as a theater director and worked as an art dealer when he couldn't earn a living in the theater. He has also been a tennis pro, a ditch digger and a salvage diver. His original plays and translations of Moliere, Aristophanes and Sophocles have been produced Off Broadway. His poetry, fiction and essays have appeared in hundreds of literary magazines and his published books include 40 poetry collections, 14 novels, 4 short story collections, 2 collection of essays and 8 books of plays. Gary lives in New York City.

Lucy Brighton is a Barnsley-based writer (between Sheffield and Leeds before you pull the map out). She teaches and writes and has ridiculous conversations with her naughty dog, Loki. Twitter Handle @brightwritenow

Paul Brucker, a marketing communications writer, lives in Mt. Prospect, IL, "Where "Friendliness is a Way of Life." He put a lid on poetry writing when he went to the Northwestern University grad ad school in a questionable attempt to learn how to think like a businessman and secure a decent income. Nevertheless, he has succumbed to writing poetry again.

He has been published recently in "Pennslyvania Literary Journal, "Wink," "The Literary Nest," "Otherwise Engaged," "The Beautiful Space," "Prachya Review," "The Bangalore Review," "monthstoyears" and "The Pagan's Muse: Words of Ritual, Invocation and Inspiration."

Paul Callus is a retired teacher who lives in Malta, Europe. He has been active in the literary field for around 50 years. He writes poetry, short stories, and lyrics for songs, mostly in English, Maltese, and Italian. His work has been published in various anthologies, journals and online sites. He is also a translator and proofreader.

Joan E. Cashin writes from Ohio, and she has published in various journals such as ARIEL CHART, SOFT CARTEL, MONO, RIGGWELTER, and WRITING IN A WOMAN'S VOICE.

Christina Chin — Malaysian artist is a widely published haiku poet. She is a four-time recipient of top 100 in the mDAC Summit Art Contests, exhibited at the Palo Alto Art Center. She is the sole haiku contributor for MusArt book of Randall Vemer's paintings. 1st prize winner of the 34th Annual Cherry Blossom Sakura Festival 2020 Haiku Contest. 1st prize winner in the 8th Setouchi Matsuyama 2019 Photo-haiku Contest.

Martin Christmas lives in Adelaide, South Australia; has a Master of Arts in Australian Cultural Studies; and is a poet, photographer, and theatre director. He has been published in Australian anthologies, and overseas in Red River Review (USA), as a Featured Poet; StepAway Magazine (UK); and Bindweed (Ireland). His poetry books are Immediate Reflections, The Deeper Inner, D&M Between 2 Men and Random Adventure (all by Ginninderra Press).

Cathleen Cohen was the 2019 Poet Laureate of Montgomery County, PA. A poet, painter and teacher, she created the *We the Poets* program for children (www.theartwell.org.) Her poems appear in several literary journals and in three collections: *Camera Obscura* (2017,Moonstone Press), *Etching the Ghost* (2021,Atmosphere Press) and *Sparks and Disperses* (2021, Cornerstone Press). Her artwork is on view at Cerulean Arts Gallery (www.ceruleanarts.com).

Jim Conwell's background is London Irish and the themes of exile and dislocation are strong in his work. He is published widely in magazines and in three anthologies. He has had two poems shortlisted in the Bridport Poetry Prize and was recently longlisted for the Brian Dempsey Memorial Pamphlet Competition. jimpconwellpoetry.com

Christopher T. Dabrowski
https://krzysztoftdabrowsk.wixsite.com/krzysztoftdabrowski
https://www.instagram.com/krzysztof.t.dabrowski/
https://www.facebook.com/Krzysztof-T-Dąbrowski-166581686751600/

Brian Daldorph teaches at the University of Kansas and the DARE Center for unhoused people. His most recent book is Words Is a Powerful Thing: Twenty Years Teaching Creative Writing at Douglas County Jail (U of Kansas P, 2021). Brian was born in Harrogate, Yorkshire.

Steve Denehan lives in Kildare, Ireland with his wife Eimear and daughter Robin. He is the author of two chapbooks and four poetry collections. Winner of the

Anthony Cronin Poetry Award and twice winner of Irish Times' New Irish Writing, his numerous publication credits include Poetry Ireland Review and Westerly.

Christine Emmert is an actress, director, writer and educator. Her work has been read/performed throughout the USA, UK and Canada. She holds a BA and MHA from the University of Colorado. Her work attempts to combine the fantasy of the mind with the actuality of living.

Alexander Etheridge has been developing his poems and translations since 1998. His poems have been featured in *The Potomac Review, Scissors and Spackle, Ink Sac, Cerasus Journal, The Cafe Review, The Madrigal, Abridged Magazine, Susurrus Magazine, The Journal, Roi Faineant Press,* and many others. He was the winner of the Struck Match Poetry Prize in 1999, and a finalist for the *Kingdoms in the Wild* Poetry Prize in 2022. He is the author of, *God Said Fire*, and the forthcoming, *Snowfire and Home.*

A recent octogenarian, **Vern Fein**, has published over 250 poems and short pieces on over 100 different sites. His first poetry book – I WAS YOUNG AND THOUGHT IT WOULD CHANGE – was published last year and a second book – REFLECTION ON DOTS – is in process.

Zary Fekete…
…grew up in Hungary
…has a novelette (*In the Beginning*) out from ELJ Publications and a debut novella being published in early 2024 with DarkWinter Lit Press.
…enjoys books, podcasts, and many many many films. Twitter and Instagram: @ZaryFekete

Danny D. Ford's poetry & artwork has appeared in numerous online and print titles. He has sixteen chapbooks to his name, including the recent collections *Rum Lime Rum* (Laughing Ronin Press 2023) and *Sucking on a Wet Pint* (Anxiety Press 2022). He can be found in Bergamo, Italy,

www.theunfoldinghead.com / @theunfoldinghead

Tim Frank's short stories have been published in Wrongdoing Magazine, X-R-A-Y Literary Magazine, Maudlin House, Rejection Letters and elsewhere. He was runner-up in The Forge Literary Flash Fiction competition '22. He has been nominated for Best Small Fictions '23.
He is the associate fiction editor for Able Muse Literary Journal and lives with his wife and child in North London, England.

Twitter: @TimFrankquill

John Grey is an Australian poet, US resident, recently published in Stand, Santa Fe Literary Review, and Lost Pilots. Latest books, "Between Two Fires", "Covert" and "Memory Outside The Head" are available through Amazon. Work upcoming in the Seventh Quarry, La Presa and California Quarterly.

Doug Hawley: The author is a little old former actuary who lives with editor Sharon and cat Kitzhaber in Oregon USA. In addition to around six hundred publications in several countries and most of the usual genres he has recently published the story collection "Weird Science" and "Vernonia Trilogy". When not writing he is probably sleeping, eating, drinking, moving, or volunteering.
Twitter: DougHawley8
Blog: https://doug.car.blog/
Website: https://sites.google.com/site/aberrantword/
Iranian Site WIP (interesting story): https://doug.ir/

Robin Ouzman Hislop's poetics cultivate a relationship between ecological processes and experimental work. He's co-authored translations of contemporary Spanish poets into English and written and performed numerous audio visual video poems. His appearances include *Cold Mountain Review (Appalachian University, N.Carolina), The Honest Ulsterman, Crátera Revista de Critica y Poesia 3, The Hypertexts.com, Better than Starbucks, Dreich Magazine, Version9Magazine, Lothlorien Poetry Journal, ImmaginePoesia, Zoetic Press* and *Bindweed Magazine*. His publications are collected poems *All the Babble of the Souk, Cartoon Molecules, Next Arrivals and Moon Selected Audio Textual Poems*. Anthologies: *Voices without Borders, Phoenix Rises from the Ashes* (a multi international anthology of sonnets), *Bark and Blossom* (an anthology of ecological poetry) and *The White Cressets Arts Journal*. Forthcoming anthologies: *Heathentide Orphans, Winter Wonderland December 2023* and *Chaucerberries Garden*. His translations from Spanish are poems by *Guadalupe Grande, Key of Mist and Carmen Crespo, Tesserae*, the award winning (*XIII Premio César Simón De Poesía*). In November 2017 works from his publications were presented in a live performance at *The International Writer's Conference* hosted by the University of Leeds. UK. He was online publisher of Poetry Life & Times at Artvilla.com for ten years. A retired TEFL teacher and translator who lives in Avila Spain and Yorkshire UK, you may visit http://www.aquillrelle.com/authorrobin.htm about author.

James Croal Jackson works in film production. His most recent chapbooks are *Count Seeds With Me* (Ethel Zine & Micro-Press, 2022) and *Our Past Leaves* (Kelsay Books, 2021). Recent poems are in *Stirring, SAND,* and *Vilas Avenue*. He edits *The Mantle Poetry* from Pittsburgh, Pennsylvania. (jamescroaljackson.com)

Erin Jamieson (she/her) holds an MFA in Creative Writing from Miami University. Her writing has been published in over eighty literary magazines, including a Pushcart Prize nomination. She is the author of a poetry collection (*Clothesline*, 2023) and four poetry chapbooks. Her latest poetry chapbook, *Fairytales,* was published by Bottle Cap Press.

Michael Lee Johnson Michael Lee Johnson , USA & Canadian citizen, now

Chicagoland area, is an internationally published poet in 45 countries, a song lyricist, has several published poetry books, has been nominated for 7 Pushcart Prize awards, and 6 Best of the Net nominations. Over 298 YouTube poetry videos as of 12-2023.

George Justice holds a B.A. in English Literature and Creative Writing. He has been published five times for short stories, three times for poetry, and was a long-time movie critic for Michigan's *Oakland County Daily Tribune*. During his enlistment with the U.S. Army, he wrote numerous articles (from human interest to military) for *Stars and Stripes*. While at the University of Detroit, he was "one-of-twelve" chosen from a field of over 300 for a semester-long advanced creative writing symposium conducted by then writer-in-residence, John Gardner. His first novel "Greezy Creek" was published in September 2019. His second novel "Edenfield" is slated for publication in June 2024.

WEBSITE: georgerobjustice.com

Suzanne Kelsey is currently permitted to share residence with her 17-year-old cat. In between brushing and feeding Miss Poo, Suzanne enjoys trying new recipes, listening to audiobooks, writing, and drinking wine. Her works have appeared in Neologism Poetry Journal, The Literary Hatchet, Night Picnic, The Chamber Magazine, 1807, Bartleby, and Children, Churches, & Daddies.

Jane Rosenberg LaForge is the author of four full-length poetry collections; four chapbooks of poetry; a memoir; and two novels. Her most recent poetry has or will appear in the *Evening Street Review; The Healing Muse*; and the *American Journal of Nursing*. She reads poetry for *COUNTERCLOCK* literary magazine and reviews books for *American Book Review*. More information is at janerosenberglaforge.com.

C.L. Liedekev is a two-time nominee for Best of the Net, with his poem, "November Snow. Philadelphia Children's Hospital," being a finalist in 2021. His work can be found at Humana Obscura, Red Fez, MacQueen's, Hare's Paw, River Heron Review, Marrow, American Writers Review, and Quibble.

Kevin MacAlan lives in rural Co Waterford in Ireland. He has an MA in Creative Writing, is a founding member of the West Waterford Arts Group, and recently contributed to The Waxed Lemon, An Áitiúil, and Howl in Ireland, Recesses in the UK, and Purple Unicorn Media in the USA.

Ben Macnair is an award-winning poet and playwright from Staffordshire in the United Kingdom. Follow him on Twitter @benmacnair

Paul McAllister was born in Northern Ireland and brought up there and in Scotland, but now lives and works far away from both. His work has previously appeared in the

Honest Ulsterman and the Belfast Telegraph, and also in a number of other outlets under various pseudonyms.

Andrew Nickerson's originally from Massachusetts, and has been an avid reader for almost 30 years. He started writing in high school, continued while earning his BA in History (English minor) at UMASS Lowell and JD at Mass. School of Law, and never looked back. He's since self-published a novella on Amazon, printed 1 article apiece on Polygon, Anime Herald, and Pipeline Artists, 2 more on Ariel Chart and Academy of Heart and Mind, and recently printed a short story in Evening Street Review's 2022 Winter Edition.

Michael G. O'Connell is an author, illustrator, and an award-winning poet. Having been published in various formats worldwide, his latest work can be found in the poetry anthology, *Moss Gossamer*. He is currently working on an illustrated middle grade book.

Charlotte Amelia Poe (they/them) is an autistic nonbinary author from England. Their first book, How To Be Autistic, was published in 2019. Their debut novel, The Language Of Dead Flowers, was published in September 2022. Their second novel, Ghost Towns, was self published in 2023. Their second memoir, Conversations With Monsters, will be published in 2024. Their poetry has been published internationally.

Twitter: @charlottepoe
Instagram: @smallreprieves
Website: charlottepoe.com

Susan L. Pollet is a published author of 11 books including one book of poetry entitled "Susiku, And More." She is also a visual artist, lawyer, world traveler, and lover of all things NYC. Her dedication to her grandchildren, her advocacy, and to her creative life, knows no bounds.

Gabriel Lukas Quinn Gabriel Lukas Quinn (he/him) is a 20-year-old gay writer and English student from Portland, Oregon. Quinn authors short speculative fiction, psychological thrillers, and poetry concerning mental health. Literature is a preservation of the soul... so write or die, y'all! Quinn has been featured in several publications such as *A Thin Slice of Anxiety, The Kings River Review, Perceptions Literary Magazine, The Sucarnochee Review*, and *The Whistle Pig Literary Journal*. Find Quinn (@ichaotiqa) on Instagram.

Dora Rollins teaches creative writing in the Tucson, Arizona, state prison where her students are also writing colleagues. She serves as an Associate Editor for the 50-year-old incarceration-focused Rain Shadow Review literary magazine. She has been published in *Wordpeace*, the *Corvus Review*, and *Right Hand Pointing*.

William Ross is a Canadian writer and visual artist living in Toronto. His poems have appeared in *Rattle, Bluepepper, Humana Obscura, New Note Poetry, Cathexis Northwest Press, Topical Poetry, *82 Review,* and *Alluvium.* Recent work is forthcoming in *Heavy Feather Review* and *The New Quarterly.*

Dr David Rudd is an emeritus professor of literature who, after some 40 years, turned from academic prose to creative writing and found contentment. Of his 50-ish stories, recent ones have appeared in "Altered Reality," "Aphelion," "Bandit Fiction," "Bewildering Stories," "The Blotter," "Corner Bar Magazine," "Dribble Drabble Review," "Jerry Jazz Musician," "Literally Stories," and "Scribble."

Terry Sanville lives in San Luis Obispo, California with his artist-poet wife (his in-house editor) and two plump cats (his in-house critics). He writes full time, producing short stories, essays, and novels. His short stories have been accepted more than 500 times by journals, magazines, and anthologies including The American Writers Review, The Galway Review, and Shenandoah. He was nominated three times for Pushcart Prizes and once for inclusion in Best of the Net anthology. Terry is a retired urban planner and an accomplished jazz and blues guitarist – who once played with a symphony orchestra backing up jazz legend George Shearing.

Gordon Scapens is widely published over many years in various countries in numerous magazines, journals, anthologies and competitions, most recently first prize in the Brian Nisbet poetry award. His book 'History Never Dies' came out this month.

Fiona Scott-Barrett lives in Edinburgh, writes fiction and non-fiction, and is partially-sighted. In June 2023 she was the runner up in the Society of Authors' ADCI Literary Prize for her debut novel, The Exit Facility.
https://www.instagram.com/fionascottbarrett/

LB Sedlacek has had poems and stories appear in a variety of journals and zines. Her poetry has been nominated for Best of the Net. Her latest poetry book is "Unresponsive Sky" published by Purple Unicorn Media. Other poetry books include "Swim," "The Poet Next Door," "This Space Available," and "Words and Bones." Her latest short stories book is "The Renovator & Motor Addiction" published by Alien Buddha Press. Other fiction books include "The Jackalope Committee and Other Tales," "The Mailbox of the Kindred Spirit," and "Four Thieves of Vinegar & Other Short Stories." LB also enjoys swimming and reading.

Leo Shtutin is a translator and writer based in London. He has translated essays and articles for online publications such as openDemocracy and The Calvert Journal. He has also translated several full-length works, including Death of a Prototype, a novel by Victor Beilis (Anthem Press, 2017), and Emergence of a Hero, an academic book by Andrei Zorin (Oxford University Press, 2023). His monograph Spatiality and Subjecthood in Mallarmé, Apollinaire, Maeterlinck, and Jarry: Between Page and

Stage was published by Oxford University Press in 2019.

Originally from Bury, Lancashire, **Damian Tarnowski** now resides in Whitby, North Yorkshire. He has three children, a girlfriend and dog and is a postie by day and writer by night.

Scott H. Urban has worked as a teacher, assistant principal, and social work case manager, but all along the way he was writing prose, poetry, and reviews. His poetry has recently been published in FALLING STAR, BURNINGWORD, THE 2 RIVERS VIEW, and ECLECTICA. His verse has been collected in the volumes NIGHT'S VOICE, SKULL-JOB, ALIGHT, and GOD'S WILL. He lives with his family in southeastern Ohio in an Amish farmhouse that isn't haunted . . . yet.

Jonathan Vidgop is a theatre director, author, screenwriter, and founder of the Am haZikaron Institute for Science and Heritage of the Jewish People in Tel-Aviv, Israel. Born in Leningrad in 1955, Jonathan was expelled in 1974 from what is now called the Saint-Petersburg State University of Culture and Arts "for behavior unworthy of the title of Soviet student." Having worked as a locksmith, loader, and White Sea sailor, he was drafted into the army and sent to serve in the Arctic Circle. He is the author of several books. Two chapters from his latest novel, Testimony, published by the leading Russian Publishing House NLO, "Birdfall" and "Man of Letters," were published in English in Goats Milk Magazine and The CHILLFILTR Review. A story was recently accepted by Los Angeles Review, and another by Pembroke Magazine. The story "Nomads" is the recent winner of the Meridian's Editors' Prize in Prose. Besides USA, Vidgop's stories were published in Israel, England, South Africa, Singapore, Russia, Japan, and Romania.

Rebecca Wheatley is an actress, singer and poet born in west London now living by the sea in Brighton with her husband and son. She tours the UK extensively writing her poetry on her way round.

Lynn White lives in north Wales. Her poetry is influenced by issues of social justice and events, places and people she has known or imagined. She is especially interested in exploring the boundaries of dream, fantasy and reality. She has been nominated for a Pushcart Prize, Best of the Net and a Rhysling Award. Find Lynn at: https://lynnwhitepoetry.blogspot.com and https://www.facebook.com/Lynn-White-Poetry-1603675983213077/

K.D. Zwierz's poems have appeared, or are forthcoming, in Poetry Pacific, Beyond Words, Tincture and Buzz, amongst others. He was featured in the anthology Ukraine in the work of international poets (Literary Waves), published in Poland, and is a co-editor at Beyond Words Literary Magazine. He lives and writes between Croatia and Kuwait.

About the Editors

Joseph Robert's poetry and fiction has appeared in magazines and anthologies worldwide. In 2016 his poetry was longlisted for the Melita Hume Poetry Prize. His two most recent poetry collections are available from Amazon and other online retailers: Brexit Brokeshit (2019) and Mastered Thesis (2021). https://josephrobert.home.blog

Leilanie Stewart is an author and poet from Belfast, Northern Ireland. She writes ghost and psychological horror, including award-winning novel, The Blue Man, as well as experimental verse. Her writing confronts the nature of self; her novels feature main characters on a dark psychological journey who have a crisis and create a new sense of identity. She began writing for publication while working as an English teacher in Japan, a career pathway that has influenced themes in her writing. Her former career as an Archaeologist has also inspired her writing and she has incorporated elements of archaeology and mythology into both her fiction and poetry.

In addition to promoting her own work, Leilanie runs Bindweed Anthologies, a creative writing publication with her writer husband, Joseph Robert. Aside from publishing pursuits, Leilanie enjoys spending time with her husband and their lively literary lad, a voracious reader of sea monster books.

www.leilaniestewart.com

SUBMISSION CALL

We are now open for submissions for our Midsummer Madness 2024 Bindweed Anthology. We're looking for poetry and prose that's offbeat or one of a kind. The anthology will be published on 21st June 2024. Even though it will be released on the solstice, there is no theme.

We're looking for poetry, fiction or other unpublished literary hybrids that are experimental, offbeat or one of a kind.

Read our full guidelines at: https://bindweedmagazine.com/submission-guidelines

Send submissions to: heavenlyflowerpublishing@gmail.com

We look forward to reading your work!

Leilanie Stewart and Joseph Robert

Printed in Great Britain
by Amazon

35611735R00092